The leering skull's mouth opened in a silent scream, a silent cry of triumph . . .

"Help me!" the man screamed, and reached a hand for the fragile broken branch of a tree.

A double-bladed axe flashed before his horror-struck eyes. There was a brief moment's pain in his wrist and he watched as his severed hand flew out across the bog, sucked below the green surface in an instant.

The darkness of unconsciousness immediately consumed him . . .

But not before he had glimpsed that blade raised once again and brought down heavily against his skull.

The blow which split him open drove his body a yard below the surface of the mud . . .

Charter books by Robert Faulcon

NIGHT HUNTER
NIGHT HUNTER 2: THE TALISMAN

coming in November:

NIGHT HUNTER 3: THE GHOST DANCE

NIGHT HUNTER
The Talisman

Robert Faulcon

CHARTER BOOKS, NEW YORK

NIGHT HUNTER 2: THE TALISMAN

A Charter Book/published by arrangement with
the author

PRINTING HISTORY
Arrow edition published 1983
Charter edition/September 1987

All rights reserved.
Copyright © 1983 by Robert Faulcon.
This book may not be reproduced in whole or in part,
by mimeograph or any other means, without permission.
For information address: The Berkley Publishing Group,
200 Madison Avenue, New York, New York 10016.

ISBN: 0-441-57475-0

Charter Books are published by The Berkley Publishing Group,
200 Madison Avenue, New York, New York 10016.
The name "Charter" and the "C" logo are trademarks
belonging to Charter Communications, Inc.

10 9 8 7 6 5 4 3 2 1

To Chris Evans, friend and fellow Celt.

ONE

Edmonton, Canada

EVENTUALLY, THE THOUGHT which she'd been fighting so hard not to acknowledge became too strong to ignore: he had met someone else, another woman. He'd had plenty of opportunity to do so during their two-week stay at the Norfolk farm. A girl from the town, or another tourist, and over the months since that holiday in England, last summer, he had slowly been going out of his mind: with distraction, with love, with loneliness.

As she trudged home from work, through the deep, crisp snow that still swathed Edmonton, Karen Seymour tried not to cry. It may have been Spring elsewhere in the world, but this far north the snows were as deep and as cold as ever; her breath frosted before her face, and any tear would turn instantly to ice on her cheeks. She was swathed in winter clothing, carrying a bag full of shopping.

Karen was a handsome woman in her early thirties, pregnant for the second time, and suffering deepening bouts of depression as well as sickness. It was a time during which she needed comfort, and the sympathetic presence of husband Jack and their four-year-old urchin of a son, Chris. Instead, Chris locked himself away with his toys and books, as depressed by the seemingly endless winter as any adult. And Jack...

Jack was going out of his mind over something. He was a

haunted, disturbed man, increasingly given to bouts of melancholy silence. For the last month they had hardly talked. And all Karen could think of by way of explanation was that he had found another woman.

Her car was out of action at the moment, and since she only worked locally she had decided that making the difficult walk to the office was all right. Jack worked miles away and needed his car for business. This afternoon she had left early, mainly because she was feeling ill, and she had picked up the shopping on the way back. She was anticipating a couple of hours with her feet up and the TV on before Jack came home, and Chris came back from the infant's school.

So when she saw Jack's car, half in, half out of the garage, she felt a sudden shock, stopped in the street and stared at her house.

He was home from work already!

But he'd had an important business meeting this afternoon, and even if that had been cancelled, Jack *never* left work before six o'clock. There were times when she wished that Jack *would* take a few hours unofficial leave, but the man was a workaholic, and to be home in midafternoon was totally untypical.

Her feelings of gloom deepened as she hastened her step, praying that no neighbours would emerge to hold her up with inane conversation about the endless snow and the possibility of yet another power cut that evening. Once inside the house she dumped her bag of shopping in the kitchen, shrugged off her bulky anorak, and walked slowly into the lounge.

Jack was there, dressed in a casual shirt and slacks, a can of beer held in one hand. He had covered the coffee table with photographs and was leaning forward in one of the deep armchairs, poring over the prints. He looked up quickly and smiled as Karen entered the room. "Karen! Hi! You're home early."

She couldn't bring herself to smile back. "*I'm* home early. I'm often home in the mid afternoon. But what are *you* doing here? What happened to the business meeting?"

But Jack paid no more attention to her, nor to her sombre face, or the way she stood just inside the door, arms folded. He picked up a photograph and stared at it. Karen could see that they were the holiday snaps from Wansham, the village in Norfolk, England, which they had visited this last summer.

"D'you remember that old church? St. Magnus's? What a place. What history . . ." he settled back in his chair, looked up at Karen. He was in his mid-thirties, receding slightly, but still dark-haired and lean of features. A handsome man, she thought. Strong. And a good father to Chris. They had done well to wait for some years before starting their family, to get settled, to know themselves more completely before accepting the responsibilities for a new life.

But what had gone wrong? What was *going* wrong? Karen could hardly bear to think, to ask the question. She had not realized the extent to which she needed Jack's strength until now. With Jack behaving so peculiarly, so out of character, she was beginning to feel increasingly lost.

"Why *are* you home so early?" Karen repeated, and Jack just shrugged.

"I took the whole week off . . ."

The words were like a blow to her. She walked into the room quickly. "You've taken the whole *week* off! What the hell for?"

Calmly he said, "Holiday. We're going back to Norfolk and I need to prepare things . . ."

"We're *what*?"

"Going back to Norfolk."

For a second she just stood and stared at him, hardly believing she had heard his words correctly. And yet it should not have been such a shock to her. His increasing obsession with last summer's holiday had made her think that it was *there* that he had met another woman; it was only natural that he should propose returning to England.

She turned from him angrily, walking to the window to stare out at the garden. "What the hell's the matter with you, Jack?" she said grimly, coldly. "What the *hell's* the matter?"

Tell me. Get it over with. Crush me now. End the agony.

"Nothing's the matter, Kay. Nothing. I've taken a week off so that we can have a quick Spring holiday. I don't understand why you seem so hostile to the idea."

She turned on him sharply. He was leaning back in the chair his face pleasant, smiling, reassuring.

She said, "Why, Jack?"

"Why what?"

"Why d'you want to go back? To England."

He shrugged, as if the answer should have been obvious. "It was a good holiday, Kay. You enjoyed it. I enjoyed it..."

She stared at him, wanting to cry. "We had a good two weeks. It was pleasant. Yes, I agree. But Jack, it wasn't *that* pleasant. It wasn't 'go again eight months later' pleasant. It wasn't another-two-thousand-dollars-of-airfare pleasant!"

Jack stood up and crossed the room to her. His dark eyes shone with an intensity that Karen read as pure, hard determination. "I've made up my mind, Karen. We're going back. Look, you'll enjoy it. We can afford a couple of thousand dollars..."

"And the farm house rent? We don't even know if they'll take us off-season..."

"They can and they will. I already rang. And we'll get a third off the weekly rate just because it *is* off-season."

"For Christ's sake..." she turned back to the window, shaking with confusion, and frustration. She wanted to tell him loudly, defiantly, that he should go on his own, then, and leave her here. But she couldn't say it. She didn't want it. She didn't want him alone in England... she might lose him for good.

Jack placed his hands on her shoulders reassuringly. "What's the matter, Kay?"

"I don't *want* to go back there. What's the point?"

"The point is," he said, an edge of anger in his voice, "the point is a holiday, a break from this godforsaken winter."

She swung around, angry. "Okay. I agree. Let's go to Hawaii. If we're going to have an extra holiday, let's go somewhere warm. Let's go to Hawaii."

"I don't want to go to Hawaii," he said, almost petulantly.

"And I don't want to go back to England! Cold, bleak, miserable bloody country!"

"I thought you'd enjoyed our stay there."

"Not that much!" Her voice was almost hysterical. There was a brief, glaring silence between them, broken by Karen, who said, "And what about Chris?"

"Your sister will look after him. You know she will. A

week, Kay. Just a brief return visit. I've *got* to go back." He frowned even as he said it, puzzled by the intensity of his words. He repeated, "I've just got to see the place again. I can't get it off my mind, Kay. I *need* to go back."

She found the courage to speak her mind, to say the thing that had begun to haunt her. "You met someone there. You met another woman. Tell me, Jack, for Christ's sake..."

"Don't keep swearing," he told her sternly. Then shook his head, smiling almost patronizingly. "Is that what you've been thinking? That I met a girl in Norfolk and am obsessed with seeing her again?"

She let him put his arms around her, hugging her to his breast. She said, "What else am I supposed to think? You've been driving me mad these last few days. Distracted, not sleeping, restless. This obsession to go back to Kett's farm, to Wansham... what else am I supposed to think?"

"But I want you to come with me, Kay. There's no other woman. I swear it. Not even Agnes Hadlee..." He grinned. Even Karen smiled at the thought of the plump, jolly farmer's wife with whom they'd stayed last summer.

She said, "Then why in God's name *do* you want to go to that bleak, miserable little town again?"

His hug grew stronger. Karen pulled back a little and she could see the uncertainty in his eyes. He shrugged, smiled thinly. "I don't know. I just... I just *have* to. It's something that's eating at me, Kay. I swear to God that there's no-one there, no woman, no man. Perhaps it's my past, something I recognized when I was there. But I've *got* to go, and you too. I want you there with me. For a week, Kay. Just one week. Just to see the place. Please..."

She broke away from him and crossed the room. She sat on the edge of an armchair and picked up two or three of the pictures: the farmhouse had been charming, she supposed, if cramped, cold and distinctly damp; it had at least been well run. It looked across flat fields towards a gentle rise, topped by sinister trees, and in the opposite direction towards the grey, unwelcoming sea. The town itself was a typical fenland village, its small supermarket the only concession to modern living. Karen could still feel the biting summer winds, the awful autumnal weather that had accompanied their trip to

Jack's parental homeland. If she were honest with herself, she had hated the holiday, and thought that Jack had disliked it too.

But at least she felt reassured about her naïve and almost childish worry over another woman.

Which left, however, another puzzle: where on earth did Jack's irrational desire come from? He was dead set on returning to England. She watched him as he stood above her, gaze half on her, half on the display of summer photographs. She could remember nothing that had occurred during the holiday which could account for his strange behaviour now—nothing, that is, except that one day, towards the end of their stay there . . .

He had walked off alone, cheerful, and returned dishevelled and upset, frozen stiff from having fallen into a boggy pond, but unable to recall exactly what had caused him to slip.

It hadn't spoiled the vacation, and she had thought no more of it. Now she remembered that odd day, and equated it with his even odder behaviour, his restless obsession with the Norfolk town.

There was no answer to be found in her scattered, confused thoughts. Reluctantly, hating herself as she said the words, she murmured, "Okay. Let's go back to Wansham. Let's get it over with."

Southampton

The more he thought about the idea, the more he liked it. A few days "off," or rather—since he was retired—a few days away.

A week, say, seven days away from the busy-body neighbours, away from the Working Men's Club, away from Monday evening bingo. A few days break from the tedium of life in Chisholm Road.

Quite when the idea had occurred to him was hard to remember now, but the exact reason for his sudden interests and equally sudden changes of mind was not something that concerned Martin Shackleford. All he knew was that one morning, perhaps it was yesterday, he had woken up at six in the morning thinking about Wansham, and that little hotel with the kindly landlady, Mrs. Quinn, and the excellent English breakfasts. He had lain in bed for several hours, just reliving those few days of holiday, last summer, when his youngest daughter Sharon had taken him on a tour of the fens and Norfolk.

Sharon was unmarried, and seemed a lonely sort of girl; she didn't get on well with her two sisters, but always enjoyed visiting Southampton for long weekends. Father and daughter were good friends, closer now that Margaret was gone, and that holiday had been a wonderful break for them both, and a chance to forge a new and very pleasant relationship. Sharon would probably never get married; it wasn't that she didn't have looks, or talent. She just seemed so wrapped up in her teaching job, and her friends, and her hobbies.

Shackleford had called the girl at her Nottinghamshire flat, but Sharon was away with friends. He had been about to suggest that they meet up at the Royal Oak hotel, in Wansham, and have a couple of days together at his expense, but it suddenly seemed like a good idea to go alone.

He had rung the hotel and confirmed his booking. He had spent the day packing his small suitcase, and arranging for his two cats to be fed by the only neighbour in the road that he actually *liked*. As the day had worn on so his excitement had grown. He couldn't get the town, and the countryside around the town, out of his mind. Those long walks along the windy embankment—the sea bluff, the locals called it—which separated farmland from the surging, unswimmable sea. The still days, the sun bright and hot, when they had walked across the farmland, following winding brooks through gnarled and wind-blasted copses of beech and oak trees. The long drive through some of the most beautiful and remote fenland imaginable.

He was up early the next day. It was cloudy, cool. An April shower threatened, and he could see by the grey, sombre sky that it would be more than the usual April downpour.

So he quickly loaded up his old Morris Traveller and scuttled back into the house to make breakfast. It was not yet seven in the morning, but soon the road would be lively with people heading off to work, and he particularly wanted to avoid the Starkeys at number 46, who would question him thoroughly, and irritate him no end.

He tried calling Sharon once more, but the phone didn't answer at all. He called her work and was told that the girl was somewhere in the Derby area, on a two-day teachers' conference.

Ah well, it had only been a passing idea, anyway.

The important thing was to get on the road and back to Wansham before the rain became too heavy. He had a good day's drive ahead of him, and he tired easily behind the wheel.

He wanted to make the town before late afternoon.

Wansham

"I must have been out of my mind to let you drag me all the way back here. Out of my mind! D'you hear me, John?"

"I hear you! And I wish I didn't have to!"

"Well, that does it! I'm going back to the hotel. *And* I'm taking the car."

John Keeton sighed with irritation and turned round to watch as his wife, Kath, walked angrily back along the pathway to where they had parked their estate car, now just visible at the side of the distant road. "Kath!" he shouted after her. "Just a few minutes more. Just a little way more!"

"Not one step!" she called back. She slipped slightly on the wet mud of the pathway and her voice was a shrill cry of fury. It was a bloody miserable day by anybody's standards. The wind was fairly whipping in off the sea, blowing reeds, trees and clothing before it. Katherine Keeton felt the cold very badly. She was nearly fifty, and liked her comforts. She was huddled inside her raincoat, now, hair held down by a green headscarf, body hunched and frozen as she worked her way back across the evil, bleak landscape.

John Keeton swore silently, then shook his head, glancing back along the bluff, out across the flatter farmland that they had been approaching, the area known locally as "the styke." He could see some sort of tented enclosure in the distance, on a ridge of land, maybe half a mile from the farmhouse. There were more sheltering trees over there, and he had been walking steadily towards them, not really knowing why, just more and more comfortable with each step he took.

The wind didn't bother him, nor the rain. Nor the cold. Which was strange, since normally they did. But since returning to Wansham, just the day before, he had felt relaxed, almost ecstatically happy at times. At dinner last night he had been more cheerful and jokey than he could remember in a long time, and Kath's grumpiness, her sense of being a partner to his mad whim, had not succeeded in getting him down. Even at breakfast he had been excited. He hadn't been able to wait to get out and walk across the desolate countryside.

Kath, it was clear, could have found a hundred things she'd prefer to have done: washing, ironing, running their small company single-handedly, raising badgers . . . *anything* rather than tramp through the freezing April weather, towards a sea that heaved and shimmered with grey contempt for the sandflats of a beach, and the unappealing coastal landscape which it might so easily swamp one day soon. All day she had complained and bickered, and become more and more tiresome.

"Why *here*? For the Lord's sake, John, why back here? Bad food, surly service, one of the most miserable holidays we've had in a long time and you want to come *back*. Even Alan thought it was a disaster. The boy didn't speak to me for a month . . ."

"Bloody hippy," snarled John Keeton at thought of his idle eldest son.

"I must have been mad to let you bring me. I must have been mad to come . . ."

"I told you, Kath. This place appeals to me. I feel a sense of belonging. I *had* to come back."

"You've going senile, more like."

He followed her, now, back along the edge of the land, kicking sullenly through the wind-whipped rye grass. Wherever he looked, across the low farmland, he could see the sombre greys and greens, the lowering sky bringing dusk that much closer. Somewhere a bird piped merrily, a curlew, he thought, and he saw its dark shape bobbing up and down on the wind.

He was not so old that he was going senile, and the words had stung him. He *had* had a mild stroke, and his left hand was still numbed and slightly hard to flex. But that had been a year ago, and he was quite fit now. He was only fifty-six. No age at all. Damn the woman. She was ageing faster than him, her face sagging, her legs becoming ropey with hardened veins.

Sometimes he doubted their reasons for staying together, but he supposed it was something to do with mutual security. She was never afraid to speak her mind, and had strong opinions on most subjects. She was intelligent, and she helped him run his small hardware business, and was the brains behind the finance. Their two sons were long since gone from home, and rarely visited, rarely seemed at ease with their parents, although Alan had been induced to come on holiday with them the summer before, when they had stayed at the Royal Oak. He got on better with Kath than with John. Keeton felt irritable about that and could not disguise his sense of frustration.

He trudged down the bluff, slipping and sliding on the wet grass. Kath was already at the car, standing there impatiently, lips pursed, arms folded across her chest for warmth. "Hurry up, if you're coming. Let's get back to the hotel at least."

For a second, staring at the pinched face, her grey eyes cold and unloving, he realized that he hated her. He hated her for interfering in everything he wanted to do, for frustrating the free spirit in him. She brought him down. She drained him of all vitality, like some horrible vampire...

And even as these violent and cruel thoughts passed through his mind he recognized that they were somehow *alien* to him, they were not him at all, not his real feelings.

But something had snared him. He was caught in a trap of anger and irritation, and the sight of the woman standing there before him was the epitome of everything that he hated in his life, the blocking, the preventing, the depressing of desire...

I love you Kath, he thought as best he could, but the words were twisted away from him, some inner demon not allowing him to recognize his true feelings for her.

She was in the way. He had to do something about that. He hated her.

But I love you, Kath. I love you...

He reached into his pockets and drew out the car keys, flinging them in her face. "Bloody go back, then. Sod off! I'm going for a walk on my own."

And he turned his back on her and began to climb back up the bluff, to the pathway above the sea. Behind him, Kath screeched her anger, noisily opened the door of the car and a moment later was driving furiously back towards the town.

Keeton never looked over his shoulder, not until the sound of the car had vanished against the gusting wind, the moaning of the air across the Norfolk landscape. He pulled the collar of his overcoat up around his neck, and tugged his trilby hat further down across his face, hunched against the wet cold but peering intently into the distance.

He had no idea where he was walking, but he increased the pace of his step, moving almost excitedly along the bluff towards a tightly packed copse of trees, where some ruined fencing told of a hidden pond, or area of bog. There was a red notice there, but he couldn't see what it said. In the distance up on the rise, he could see a landrover moving towards the roadway that led into Wansham.

It was quite dark; late afternoon, and the stormy skies made it seem like well after dusk. Ahead of him he thought he saw a light, a brief flare against the trees.

He was compelled to drop down from the high path to the soggy ground at the edge of the farmland. His feet sank in the mud and he trudged up towards the trees, and the shelter that they offered. He was vaguely aware that the red sign was painted with the word DANGER. He was also aware that someone was lurking in that dark path of woodland, watching him.

Keeton stepped across the ramshackle fencing, and leaned against one of the gnarled trunks, peering into the gloom. The wind almost carried away his words: "Hello? Someone there?"

A flurry of rain blew cold and uncomfortable against his back and he shivered and stepped forward a little. There was movement behind him and he turned and glimpsed a human figure slipping out of sight into the copse. Puzzled, Keeton stepped among the trees, holding his coat closed at the neck, using his left hand to keep his balance by leaning against the sloping trunks.

"I've come back . . ." he called, and part of him questioned that strange statement; and yet, without really thinking at all, he called again. "It's Keeton. I'm back."

"Glad you could make it, Keeton." The voice came from the right and Keeton glanced that way.

An old man stood there, watching him. He leaned on a heavy, gnarled stick, his other hand in the pocket of a faded tweed suit. He was smiling broadly. In the half-light his eyes gleamed, almost with amusement.

Keeton took a step towards him. "Who are you?"

The old man shrugged, his gaze never leaving Keeton's face. "Who am I?" He chuckled. "Why Mister Keeton, I'm the man who called you."

"Called me?" Keeton frowned.

"You have something that I want."

"What could I possibly . . . what do I have? I don't understand."

"You have something that belongs to me, Mister Keeton, and it's time to give it back . . ."

"I have nothing . . ." an edge of panic in his voice. The old man's smiling face seemed to swim large before him, the permanent grin an almost evil thing, the twinkling, amused eyes fixing him with an animal stare. Keeton backed away, stumbling slightly as his foot caught the twisted root of a tree. Rain drove into the copse, cold and hard.

"I have nothing that belongs to you. I never saw you before."

"Why Mister Keeton, that's just not true. You took it from me last summer . . ." the old man limped uneasily after the retreating figure of John Keeton. Keeton glanced towards the unseen sea, to where the grass on the high path waved in the stormy winds. He wished that Kath had waited. The menace that exuded from this old man was terrifying . . .

"I was on holiday . . ." Keeton stammered, and his words

turned instantly to a scream. The solid ground had vanished from beneath his feet.

Panic-stricken, he yelled, "I'm sinking!" Oozing mud sucked at his legs. He struggled and twisted, but between one step and the next he had trodden in the rain-soaked bog and had sunk above the knees.

A fleeting, shocking image, held down beneath the water, struggling, staring up as he drowned into the leering face of the man who pushed him under ...

"My God," he shrieked aloud. "I can't move!"

The old man leaned close and his face rippled and transformed. Keeton watched the hideous transmogrification, his mouth gaping, the breath hardly able to express itself from his body. The old man's face seemed to grin at him, a leering skull, its mouth opening in a silent scream, a silent cry of triumph. The crippled body shimmered grey, ghostly, the limbs swelling, seemingly clad in ragged furs and clothes; muscles pushed hugely against the tenuous fabric of the robe. Long hair framed the skull that peered at the sinking man in the bog.

"Help me!" screamed Keeton, and reached a hand for the fragile broken branch of a tree.

A double-bladed axe flashed before his horror-struck eyes. There was a brief moment's pain in his wrist and he watched as his severed hand flew out across the bog, sucked below the green surface in an instant.

The darkness of unconsciousness immediately consumed Keeton ...

But not before he had glimpsed that blade raised once again and brought down heavily against his skull.

The blow which split him open drove his dead body a yard below the surface of the mud.

Two

MID MORNING OF an overcast day in late April, Andrew Haddingham returned to the house on Brook's Corner for the first time in a week. He parked his car on the grass verge by the road and switched off the engine. Leaning slightly across his passenger he surveyed the high, red brick wall, with its wrought-iron gates, that effectively blocked all view of the house itself.

"Here we are," he said. "Brook's Corner. Dann Brady's castle keep."

"I thought you said the place was defended," said the woman who sat with him, frowning slightly.

"It is. Very effectively." Haddingham knew she was referring to the fact that the gates were unlocked and swinging free. She was looking for tangible barricades, but it was not against the attack of anything physical, such as a man, that Daniel Brady had fortified his detached residence in the past month. It was not fear of physical attack that dictated the life of the reclusive man who lived within.

Haddingham stepped from the car and held the door for his passenger. Her name was Angela Huxley. She was in her early forties, and quite attractive, Haddingham thought. She was unmarried, and seemed greatly contented to remain that way. She was well-groomed, and carried herself with a stiff, English properness, wearing colourful, but highly functional clothes, reflecting her generation.

It was her face that Haddingham found most remarkable.

There was a touch of the Romany about her, her eyes and features dark, her hair, once jet-black, now streaked through with mystic—Haddingham thought beautiful—silver strands.

It was a highly appropriate look, Haddingham had decided, for Angela Huxley was a medium, and a psychic adept of very great reputation. She had worked, over the years, both with the Ennean Institute of Paranormal Research, and for the Ministry of Defence station at nearby Hillingvale, which also was devoted to paranormal studies, and which was where Haddingham himself held a good position.

Haddingham took Angela Huxley's arm and guided her across the road, a mannerism quite typical of the fifty-year-old bachelor. Angela smiled wanly to herself, but allowed him to escort her in this fashion. Everything about Haddingham was courteous, British and fussy, from his three-piece suit, so well pressed and so frayed at the cuffs, to the short briar pipe that poked from his breast pocket. He was a mysterious man, and Angela was intrigued by him as she had been on the first occasion that they had met, a week ago, when he had asked her about her availability for some "private research."

"What sort of research?" she had asked him, and had instantly noticed the way Haddingham had become cagey.

"Spirit contact," he had told her. "Quite straightforward, except that the spirits are—or might be—quite unusual. I'll explain in greater detail when you've met Dan Brady himself."

She had frowned; the name had been familiar to her, and she had said as much to Andrew Haddingham. Haddingham's eyebrows rose slightly. Seated in one of the plush armchairs that filled the dark, richly furnished lounge of her house, he drew easily on his pipe.

"I wondered if it might be," he said. "Familiar, I mean."

"Who is he? Who is Daniel Brady?"

"He's a . . ." Haddingham paused and smiled thinly. "Well, he calls himself the Night Hunter. He worked with me, once, at Hillingvale. Standard paranormal research. Very dull. But something happened a few months ago that made him leave work and become just that. A hunter. A tracker. He's hunting, now, away in the north, but I think he'll be back soon . . ."

"Mister Haddingham . . . Andrew . . ." Angela Huxley

smiled easily. "You're not making very much sense."

Haddingham acknowledged that. "I'm sorry." He peered at her narrowly, as if deciding how much to tell her, then abruptly came to a decision, leaned forward in his chair and said, "A few months back Dan Brady was viciously attacked. Savagely attacked. It happened one evening, two or three days before Christmas. It was a cold-blooded, brutal assault on him and on his wife and two young children. Dan Brady himself was left for dead. He recovered only quite recently. But his wife, Alison, and the children—a girl called Marianna, and an older boy called Dominick—had vanished. Whoever attacked them on that night stole the three of them. Took them away. Dan has no idea where. I'm sure you can imagine that he is both frantic and utterly determined to find them again."

For a second Angela Huxley said nothing, merely stared at her guest, the frown on her face deepening as she intuited the horror and fear of the events that Haddingham had so briefly described. "Poor man," she whispered finally, then added, "And in case they are dead, he wishes me to try and contact them. Do I understand that?"

"That's part of it," agreed Haddingham. "But Brady is convinced that they are alive. It's not just that he refuses to accept their deaths. He has had hints, messages, clues, if you like. He believes them to be alive; but time is running out. Basically, Angela, he doesn't know where to look for them, where to start looking, where to go. But you may be able to help. You may be able to put him in touch with someone who can help..."

She rose from her chair and crossed to her desk, where she leafed through her diary thoughtfully. Closing the book, she said, "I shall make myself available at your call, Andrew. There is nothing here that can't be rescheduled. I'll do everything I can to assist."

Thus it was that a few days later she arrived at the open gates of Brook's Corner, and walked slowly through into the fortified grounds.

She could not have been aware of the nature of the defences that Brady had built; Haddingham had given her no clue beyond the simple fact that the house was "defended." But as she reached a point, some ten yards beyond the high wall, she suddenly stopped, gasping aloud and turning quickly round, staring at Haddingham through wide eyes.

"It's gone!" was all she said, and the look on her face was fleetingly of panic, then of puzzlement.

"What's gone?" asked Haddingham as he watched her. She touched a hand to her face, then her head, her brow creasing with anxiety. And suddenly she grasped the point. "Defences! Psychic defences! Of course..."

"Can you detect them?"

Angela shook her head. "Only by the absence of noise. That's what I call the sensation in my head, the presence of spiritual matter in the atmosphere. It's like a rushing sound, very distant. It just suddenly went. Just as I reached this spot here." She stared down at the pathway, noticing that the gravel had sunk slightly, as if an object was buried there.

Haddingham said, "You've just entered the *zona magnetica*. It's the third line of defence around the house, a series of clay and iron gargoyles buried about twelve inches down..."

"It's powerful," she said, looking around the garden. The bare branches of the trees cut dark patterns against the grey sky. The grounds were deserted and quiet, and most unnerving of all was the sudden silence in her mind. She shivered. "But I shan't be able to make contact in the house. You do understand that, don't you?"

"Of course. That's not why you're here."

He took her arm and walked her slowly along the drive, towards the front door. He briefly explained the way the defences were set up around the grounds.

The high brick wall was itself a psychic defence zone, a Talisman Wall that extended around the garden. The talismans and seals that had been built into the body of the wall were mostly Roman mosaic tiles from a fragment of flooring that had been found below the southern end of the garden; the tiles had a residual power, perhaps because someone had died in that ancient house nearly two thousand years before, and that power had been turned to Dan Brady's favour.

Inside the Talisman Wall was the Line of Reflection, designed to bounce back any psychic substance that might get past the talismans, psychic substance of the sort associated with psychic attack...

But the first real line of defence was the *zona magnetica*, which had so effectively blocked Angela Huxley's subconscious contact with the spirit world outside the grounds.

The two most powerful lines of defence were the *zona mandragora* and the *mazon*. The first of these appeared as a series of bronze braziers, containing a dark mix of pungent herbs, mostly black mandrake. When lit, the organic emission from the smouldering mix was a tangible blockage to psychic projection. The *mazon* was a line of complex earth mazes, carved into the turf and concrete around the walls of the house. The most potent of psychic forces which might penetrate this far would be trapped by the intricate spirals and circles of these mazes, and ultimately dissipated.

Brook's Corner was a fortress. An ordinary man could walk in through the gates and burn the house down, but elemental forces of evil, or of the mind, any such denizens of the spirit world would find their passage to the house almost impossibly difficult.

"He is not afraid of the *men* who attacked him, that night," Haddingham said as they waited for Brady to answer the door. "He would welcome their coming back to try to finish the job..."

Angela shivered. She had heard of psychic attack, the terrible way a man or a woman could be strangled or crushed by the unseen projection of a powerful mind. She said, "But *they* won't return. Instead they're sending elementals against him..."

"They've sent one, and he destroyed it. They will almost certainly send another."

There was a noise inside the house. A moment later the door opened and Angela Huxley gained her first good look at the haunted man she had come to help.

The brutality of the physical attack upon him last December, and the anguish of the last few weeks, during which he had lived with the knowledge of the loss of his wife and family, had put a strain on Daniel Brady that was clearly marked, now, in both his face and bearing.

He was a tall man and if, a few months ago, he had been declining into middle-aged chubbiness, that had now gone; he was lean and lithe, his body seeming almost too wiry, fragile; and yet he was able to move with the speed and strength of an animal. When he shook hands with Angela Huxley the grip was gentle, but the woman intuited an immense power behind that courteous touch. He was unshaven, the dark growth of beard partially grizzled. He smiled easily, but the gesture vanished from his face as quickly as it had come. His eyes were deep and piercing, lined at the corners and heavy, below, with fatigue. Angela thought they were animal eyes, cold eyes, and she felt uncomfortable beneath their scrutiny, distracted by the anger in the glance, yet the easy smile—something false —upon his lips.

Brady knew that his appearance had changed. There was nothing he could do about it. He had aged about ten years in the brief few months of the New Year; at least, he had aged in the grey that streaked his hair and beard, and the lines that creased his pale features. In another way he had become rejuvenated; his appetite was splendid, and yet each morning the flesh and muscle of his wiry frame hugged the bones more firmly, more sparsely. It was as if he was creating the appropriate body for the newly acquired mentality of a hunting animal.

He awoke every morning, shortly before dawn. He couldn't bear to stay in bed, and would prowl through the defence zones of his garden, often naked, enjoying the dewy chill of this earliest of hours. He awoke each morning in the middle of a violent and terrifying dream, and each day the dream was the same, a memory of an evening that had begun with a family, united in the simple act of preparing for Christmas day, an evening of loving togetherness that had ended with the family carried off into the frozen darkness, a family shattered by an incomprehensible force of evil, one alone left to struggle back from the grasping hands of Death.

Images that haunted him: of an amulet, like a screaming, severed head, that had gazed blindly at him from one of his at-

tacker's necks; of a jewelled phallus, its head like a horned animal, used with brutal effect upon Alison; of a convoluted labyrinthine pattern; of a face like the walking dead . . . of a name: Magondathog. An incomprehensible name that still screamed at him, tested him, jeered at him, speaking to him from a time long gone when its subtle meaning would have been too obvious for words . . .

Brady led the way into the lounge and watched as Angela Huxley walked slowly around the edge of the room, stopping by the bureau and peering down at the small display of photographs there. Haddingham said nothing. The room was cold, almost bleak despite its furnishings. Brady saw the woman pick up a photograph of Marianna and stare at it . . .

She had found enough snow still lurking beneath two logs to make a snowball, and she crept up behind her father and threw it so that it exploded against the back of his head; she scampered, pursued, across the garden, climbing onto the roof of the woodshed with a nimbleness that almost seemed impossible in view of her cumbersome boots, and the massive anorak that swathed her tiny body. Standing there, just out of reach of him, she had thumbed her nose and laughed at him, eyes twinkling behind the small round lenses of her glasses. It was an image that would remain with him through the nightmare to come, an image of such innocence, of such childish beauty, that he reached his arms towards her and caught her as she jumped from safety into the greater security of his grasp.

"My daughter," he said to Angela Huxley. "Her name is Marianna."

"She's a beautiful child," said the woman. "And this must be Dominick . . ."

Shy Dominick. Tall and ungainly, and so terribly shy. And yet such a strong little man, so protective towards his parents, so loving . . .

He kept just three photographs in the room, three pictures to remind him of what he had lost, three images to give him the strength to begin the hunt for them again. The photograph of Alison was his favourite of her, taken two years before at a friend's wedding. Her hair fell naturally across her beautiful face and she was looking at him, almost coyly, almost invitingly; there was just the hint of a smile upon her lips. There was more than a hint of love in the way she looked at Brady, who had taken the picture.

"Your wife was a very beautiful woman," said Angela.

"She still is," Brady said sharply. "She's still alive."

Angela Huxley looked slightly embarrassed, placing the photograph back on the bureau and turning to look at the solemn man before her. "Yes, of course. I'm sorry..."

Brady smiled thinly, beckoned her to a chair. "No need. I should be the one to apologize. I didn't mean to be so short with you. There are times when I really have to convince myself that my children, that Alison, that they *are* still alive. I get very defensive about it. I have very little to go on; the dying words of a man who might have said anything to try and save his life. And a conviction. A sixth sense. A natural sort of knowing... do you understand what I mean?"

"I think so." Angela Huxley had folded her hands in her lap, and looked puzzled, now, glancing around the stark lounge. "I thought... I don't know, there was something, there *is* something..." she broke off and laughed, almost embarrassed. Haddingham stood by the French windows, watching her.

"Something here? Something in the room?" he asked.

"Yes," she said quickly. "Outside the house the sound of the spirit world was abruptly cut off. *Inside* I sense a very weak spiritual presence. I thought it might have been Alison ... but it couldn't be..."

Brady exchanged a look with Haddingham, even managed a slight smile of triumph. "Not Alison," he said. "Another friend of ours..."

Angela Huxley seemed to grasp why she had been asked to come here, to Brook's Corner. "I see. She died in this room..."

"Very violently. A few weeks ago."

"And you think she may be trapped in the house."

"She *chose* to be trapped," said Brady evenly. Angela frowned as she watched him.

"How can you know that?"

"Her name was Ellen Bancroft. It was she who devised the

defences around the house. She was an expert on psychic self-defence. She'd made herself so after an attack on her and her family identical to the attack on me and mine. Without her, Miss Huxley, I would be a dead man. I owe her an immense debt of gratitude, but I never got the chance to repay that debt..."

"Was she killed resisting psychic attack?"

"Yes. Horribly. But she had set up a snare for the thought-form, and she chose to trap herself within it. She chose to remain here."

Angela Huxley looked slightly disturbed by that. "Why would she want to do such a thing?"

"She wants to help," said Brady. "She wants revenge just as I want revenge. I am now the agent of her revenge, and she may be able to help. The only trouble is..."

"You can't *communicate* with her. I understand."

Brady nodded. "I need to know that it isn't just an echo, a conventional haunting. The woman died. The house is partly stone-built. There is a residual power in the house, but is it intellectual? Is it spiritual, or merely disanimate energy?"

He reached for a small mirror and held it towards Angela, who took it, peered at it, then at its back. "Image contact?" she asked.

"Occasionally, yes. Just the glimpse of a shadowy female shape, usually when I'm looking *away* from the mirror. And this. But is it enough?" He passed several sheets of paper on which appeared an inky scrawl. Angela looked at each sheet thoroughly. Most of them were covered with repeated words:

Dandandandandan. Ellennnnelelelelelennnn. Coldddcolddcolddandandancoldcold.

"You wrote these yourself?"

Brady said, "I supplied the pen and the hand. Something else did the writing."

"She sounds shocked," said Angela. "Violent death followed by a trapping. I imagine the spirit is shocked, disoriented."

Haddingham said, "It might also be the *echoing* effect of a violent death. That's what we need to find out. Is Ellen *trying* to communicate?"

They all moved to the table, which now stood to one side of the lounge, and sat around it, the sheets of psychic writing spread out before them. Brady watched the medium as she composed herself. He was impressed by the woman, and reminded himself that, during her work for the Institute of Paranormal Research—where Ellen Bancroft had been employed—she had encountered at least *one* unidentified spirit presence that had directed a message to "Dan."

Tell Dan. They are Awakening. Tell him. Tell Dan.

There had been other messages, and over and over again, through medium contact and psychic writing, there had been the communicating of the idea of "Awakening" and "Gathering." Not all the messages had been addressed to "Dan." But Haddingham had remembered reading transcripts of two seance sessions in which that name had been used. Each time the medium had been Angela Huxley.

As Brady himself had said, it was a long jump from "Dan" to "Daniel Brady of Brook's Corner," but Haddingham, for one, was in no doubt that something from the world of the dead was urgently trying to contact Brady (and had been so doing for a year) and it was a belief that Brady, too, had come to accept.

They are Awakening. They are reaching. Tell Dan . . .

But *who* was Awakening?

Angela Huxley was powerful, there was no doubt in his mind about that fact. Just to look at her filled him with a welcome confidence. Her eyes were never still; she saw everything, and she saw beyond the hard and fast, black, white and colourful realm of the present. When she turned those dark eyes on Brady he felt fixed to the chair, watched, surveyed, almost interpreted by her.

And yet he could tell that she, in turn, was slightly in awe of him. She was slightly nervous in his presence, slightly uneasy in keeping eye contact.

"A mirror image," she said, "and writing . . . anything else? Any other tentative contact?"

"Soon after she died," Brady said, "I heard a garbled whispering. It was strongest from the mirror . . . this mirror. She was trapped *in* the mirror; or perhaps she used the glass just as a means of containing her spirit in the house. In any event, I heard whispering. Meaningless sound, but clear enough to suggest a woman's voice. Sometimes doors open and close; someone kissed me on the lips. Just once. About a week ago."

Haddingham reacted to that with just the hint of a smile. "Was it Ellen? Were the lips Ellen's lips? Can you tell one set of lips from another?" He glanced at Angela. "A ghostly kiss. Is that common?"

She waved him silent. Brady added, for Haddingham's benefit, "I might have dreamed the lips. They certainly weren't yours."

"It does sound to me," said Angela, "as if Ellen is surfacing from death. The spirit is here, and is orienting itself. But it may be that she will never be able to communicate coherently to you. In dreams, say. The writing, if she has begun that way, is the obvious means of contact. Take up the pencil. With me here we may be able to summon her more forcefully."

Brady picked up the pencil that she had passed to him, and drew a sheet of paper towards him. Frowning, he said, "Wouldn't it be better to channel her contact through you? You *are* the medium..."

"It's not necessary," said Angela with a light smile. "I can't always be here. But my function can be to assist the spirit to find its voice. If Ellen *is* around, then she's trapped *outside* the Hinterland—that's what I call the nearest plane of the after-life. She hasn't gone onwards, but she hasn't discovered, yet, how to return to the earthly plane. I think she's very lost, very frightened. Hold the pencil ready."

"Shall we hold hands?" Haddingham whispered after a moment, but Angela Huxley shook her head. She closed her eyes. Brady closed his own eyes and thought as hard, and as affectionately as possible, of the woman who had died.

For perhaps four minutes there was silence in the room, save for the gentle breathing of the three occupants and the gusting of the wind outside. Very softly, then, Angela called Ellen's name. Three times she murmured, "Ellen! Ellen, come through to us. We're here with you, Ellen. Ellen Bancroft, come through to us."

On the third occasion that she whispered this invocation, Brady felt his left hand gently lifted and placed back on the table. He kept his eyes closed, felt the hair on his body stand on end, a reaction of fear, perhaps, or anticipation.

"I can feel her," he said aloud. "She touched my hand."

"Keep your eyes closed," whispered Angela. "Let your body go limp. Let her use you. I can feel her in the room. She's stronger..."

Again: "Ellen, come through to us. We're waiting for you."

A gentle breath on his face, warm breath, sweet. Brady didn't dare to open his eyes. He couldn't bear the reality of seeing nothing. The breath was the ghostly touch of Ellen Bancroft, but the image in his mind was of Alison... Alison, close again, Alison, in the room with him...

The fingers of his hand went cold. His left arm tingled; electric. The pencil moved in his feeble grip, the soft lead marking out pale words on the white paper.

frightdanafraidcolddan.

Angela said, "Ellen—Ellen—are you able to see beyond?"

Brady's hand moved: *Yesnoyes Yes Yes No Unclear Grey Movement Zonesblocking Break Coldcoldcold Notimenotimejustdaysjustdays Danmylovemylovecoldcoldalonealone*

Brady whispered, "Ellen... Ellen, it's Dan. This is Dan. Ellen, where do I go? Tell me where to go. Can you see them? Arachne! The collectors! Can you see them? Where do I go, Ellen. You must help me..."

But although the pressure on his hand increased for a moment, it abruptly went away. He felt suddenly clearheaded, cold, alert. Opening his eyes he saw Haddingham regarding him curiously. Angela Huxley seemed to acknowledge that Ellen Brancroft's spirit had faded for a while, but she nodded her head in a silent affirmation of something she had considered. She reached for the paper and read the jumble of words, frowning slightly.

Brady was enlivened. "She *is* here. She said to break the zones if she is to see beyond. *Is* that what she said?"

Angela was thoughtfully quiet for a moment, then glanced up quickly as if she had just realized that Brady was talking to her. "Hmm? Oh yes; certainly. The house is very effectively blocked against any and all contact Beyond. That probably helped her remain here. But if she stays linked to the house, and thus to the *earth* . . ." she leaned forward as she spoke, emphasizing the words as if she were lecturing, "then I think she will have a very limited view of the higher realms. She may not be able to tell you if Alison, or your two children, are actually there."

Brady sat back in his chair and stared at the photographs on the bureau. *But there're not there. I know that. That's not why I need Ellen Bancroft. I have to know where to look, where to go, where to start . . .*

Angela Huxley tapped a finger on the page of psychic writing that Brady had just produced. "She says she's cold—"

Haddingham shrugged. "Is that bad?"

"I think so. When a spirit says it's cold, it is uncomfortable with being summoned. Not *always*, you understand, but sometimes. She also says, 'No time, no time.' I believe that means she is already aware of beginning to slip onwards. Beyond." She met Brady's gaze. "It might also mean that time is running out for your family . . ."

"Yes," said Brady, "I'd already thought of that."

"If it *does* relate to Ellen herself, however, I'm afraid there's nothing I can do about it. The house cannot hold her. Whatever the nature of the snare she set up, I don't think it's strong enough to hold her for many weeks. So you must use her quickly, and prudently."

"I understand," said Brady evenly. "But she's here. It *is* Ellen. This is not an echo, a memory. This is real . . ."

"It's real," Angela agreed. "She must have been a remarkable woman."

She was. And she is. Thank God, for you Ellen Bancroft. And I swear I shall give you release as soon as I can.

Angela Huxley rose from the table and buttoned up her coat. She imagined that her job here was done. Through the strange channels of her mind, through her focussing presence in the room, the ghost that resided at Brook's Corner had been induced to emerge from the borders of the Hinterland. From now on it was up to Brady himself.

She said, "If you have no further use for me, gentlemen..."

But Brady remained where he was, watching her, and after a moment she sat down again, looking slightly puzzled. "You *do* have further use for me..."

"One thing more," said Brady. "If you don't mind. If you're willing. Just one thing more."

Three

AS SHE HAD feared and expected, England was every bit as dreary, overcast, and just downright depressing as the mental picture she had held before leaving Edmonton. During the flight, her spirits had been raised slightly. Flying above the cloud, she had almost been able to convince herself that the bright blue sky, the brilliant sun, would persist all the way to ground level.

But the cloud layer was half a mile deep over Heathrow, and Karen Seymour's first glimpse of earth was of a landscape battered by squally rain, miserable and grey below the endlessly dark, stormy skies.

"Oh God," she breathed, leaning back in her seat as the plane bumpily touched down. "I don't think I can cope with this..."

Her husband, sitting next to her, said, "Don't be so defeatist. So it's raining today. So what. This is *England*. This is where it began. We'll be in Wansham tomorrow and it'll be like old times, Kay. You just wait and see."

Karen stared at him, shaking her head. Jack was seated by the window, peering out across the desolate expanse of the runway, towards the sombre airport buildings. The plane was taxiing gently towards its turning point. He was smiling, he was almost trembling with excitement, eyes wide, fingers drumming out a merry beat on his knee.

He couldn't wait to get there.

Karen felt like crying. His behaviour was totally irrational, and completely out of character. As they made ready to gather their cabin luggage she glanced at him, and he was like a child on its way to the beach, all glowing anticipation and irresponsibility.

Her stomach clenched, and she felt slightly sick. She touched her smoothly rounded belly gently, praying that this madness would not affect the child who grew within her.

Dear God, let there be some simple explanation . . . Don't let him be going mad.

It was late in the afternoon in England, and Wansham was a good half-day's drive away by the car they intended to hire. They caught the underground to Gloucester Road and struggled with their overpacked case to a small hotel which had been recommended to them. It was not cheap, but it was comfortable. Karen lay down on the bed, feeling dizzy, apprehensive and just slightly sick. Jack Seymour changed and showered and then sat down with a map of East Anglia.

Outside, the rain stopped. Jack plotted their route from London, then up via Cambridge, and across the fens.

At eight o'clock they went to a hamburger restaurant to snatch a meal. Karen sat in sullen, uncomfortable silence, but Jack talked constantly, reminiscing about the previous summer's holiday, enthusing about the local history of the place. Eventually Karen's nerves frayed to the extent that she slapped her hands to her ears and shouted, "Stop it! Stop it!"

Jack looked startled, watched her as she cried. The restaurant went silent, people turning to regard the source of the outburst.

"What on earth's the matter?"

"You! You're the matter! I must have been mad to come with you. You're *mad*, Jack. You're not right . . ."

She stood from the table, grabbed her coat and began to run back to the hotel. Jack quickly paid the bill and followed her, calling her name, but she was fleet-footed and almost hysterical, and she was in the room and slouched dejectedly on the bed before he caught up with her.

He stood just inside the room, leaning against the door, staring at Karen. "Do you want to ring Chris?"

She looked up at him, eyes smeared and bleary with tears. Her lower jaw trembled, but she fought to prevent herself crying again. She looked very frail, very vulnerable sitting there, and Jack, for an instant, felt great sympathy for her, great love, great concern...

And then it was as if a hand had reached out and drawn a veil across her.

His attitude hardened. He suddenly saw her as a weak, trembling woman, a nuisance, an interference.

He hardly knew where the words came from: "You'd do anything to stop me going back! Wouldn't you. *Wouldn't you*!"

The anger in his voice startled Karen, who was suddenly less tearful, more puzzled. Through wide eyes she stared at her husband, her hands clasped in her lap. Jack felt the anger bubble within him. He walked towards her, and part of him wanted to slap out at her, to teach her not to interfere. He felt his arm go tense, realized he had clenched his fist and was looming over his wife in a very threatening way.

"What is it, Jack?" she said simply. "For God's sake tell me what's going on with you."

"Don't interfere! I'm warning you..."

Where does that come from? Why am I so angry? The rational, reasonable thought cut through the surging anger and calmed him. He smiled at Karen, then frowned. "I'm uptight about something," he said softly, and turned from her, walking to the window to stand and peer out at the lamplit, rain-slick streets.

"Well, that's obvious enough," said Karen. "Jack, this whole trip is... well, weird. We've spent over two thousand dollars to come to England, seven or right months after we were last here. That's not the behaviour of normal, rational people. I'm here because you asked me to come. But you're here... *why* are you here? I just don't know, Jack. You can't give me any sensible reason at all..."

"We're here," he said, "and that's all there is to it." He kept his back to Karen. "I told you, Kay. I *needed* to come back. Haven't you ever needed to do something? Needed to do it so bad that you couldn't think of anything else, couldn't work, couldn't sleep, couldn't concentrate?"

She stared at his broad back, at the way he stood, hands in the pockets of his slacks, figure slim and strong. "Yes," she said. "Just once. I'd met a man called Jack Seymour, and I needed him to love me in the same way I'd fallen in love with him..."

Jack turned round, stared at his wife, then smiled. He came over to her and sat down on the bed beside her, reaching for her body and holding her tightly to him.

"I thought you wanted to come," he said. "I thought I'd convinced you."

"You must be joking. I think you'd convinced yourself that I wanted to go back to Wansham. But that's all."

"Nevertheless, you're here."

She pulled back from him, pushed aside a lock of his brown hair from where it had fallen across his forehead. It was a simple, gentle touch, but he jerked back, as if she had attacked him. Immediately relaxed again, he smiled awkwardly.

Karen said, "I'm here because it was easier to be here than not to be here. It's not the expense, Jack... I know you've done well, and we're comfortably off. I don't mind that, the money. It's just that it makes no sense to come dragging back to that godforsaken landscape when we hadn't particularly enjoyed ourselves the first time we were there. I had thought," she added quietly, "as I said to you before, I had thought there was a woman..."

"No woman," he repeated. "That's not my scene. I love the woman I've got. And the little woman too, if that's going to be a girl..." he patted her slightly enlarged stomach, but the gesture, and his words, were echoes, hollow-sounding affection.

"I also wonder if you've cracked," Karen persisted, glad of this moment of communication. "You've been under a strain, Jack, no doubt about it. I really wish you'd done as I said, and gone to see Doctor Williams..."

He was softly reassuring. "There was no need to see him, because my mind is okay. I haven't cracked under pressure, of work or anything. Certainly not of work." His dark eyes glittered, and the look he gave her was almost searching, then slightly puzzled. "I'm not mad," he said. "I'm really not. It's just that..." looking away, but the grip on her hand growing stronger, "there's someone there. At Wansham. It's all I can think of, someone there who needs to *tell* me something."

"Who?"

"Oh God, I've no idea. It's a feeling, a terrible, irresistible feeling that someone wants to speak to me. Perhaps I met someone last time we were there . . ."

"You were off on your own a fair bit . . ."

"That's true. I don't actually remember everything I did. You know what it's like with holidays, everything condensing into a few intense memories. But there *was* a day . . ."

He drifted off, shaking his head. Karen thought to herself, yes, the day you came back drenched and muddy, and very distressed. "When you fell in the pond . . . is that the day you mean?"

He shrugged, raised her hand to his lips and kissed her fingers. "I can't remember much about it," he said. "I'd been walking across that place they call the styke; there were some people working near to a barn, and I remember passing by them . . . and the next thing I remember I was slipping into that muddy water, quite a long way away. Someone helped me out, but we hardly exchanged words at all. He was an old man, on holiday too, I think. We spoke very little. I was too annoyed at being such a mess."

"But you think that you have unfinished business . . ."

"I'm sure of it."

Karen nodded thoughtfully, pleased that at least Jack was actually *talking* about his obsession. "What are we talking about here? Some sort of supernatural calling? Psychic wavelengths? Or do you mean that you're guilty because you started something in Wansham and didn't finish it, and you just feel impelled to go back and finish what you started?"

Jack Seymour sighed, and smiled at his wife. "Kay, I really have no idea. I'll have a better idea when we get back to East Anglia. This trip is important to me. I can't explain it, just believe me. It's important."

Karen climbed off the bed and went to the bathroom, to prepare herself for sleep. Jack lay back across the covers and closed his eyes.

He felt an overwhelming loneliness. It had surfaced before, several times during the preceding weeks. An awesome, agonizing loneliness, and the only relief had been found in fond thoughts of the flat, silent landscape of the coast near Wansham, the dark fields, the scattered copses of gnarled, windbroken trees, the winding streams, the sea that reached away to the north, to the north...

A glimpse of the dream again, the waking dream that had haunted him—of running across that landscape, through the darkness... someone running with him...

Karen was right. Part of him could acknowledge that simple fact: that Karen was right to say that what he was doing was irrational, out of character... almost the act of a madman. But each time those thoughts surfaced he felt the loneliness again, and the commitment to return to the north. He was drawn to the village. He *needed* the village. He needed what rested there, he needed the comfort and the support that he would find there. And if Karen got in his way, if she interfered, if just *once more* she tried to prevent him from going home, then he would kill her, he would kill her with his own two hands... he would *kill* her!

"NO!"

His cry brought Karen from the bathroom. "What is it? Jack, what is it?"

But he said nothing, just cradled his face in his hands, palms blocking his eyes so that he would not see her. "Nothing..." he said, "nothing at all..." and fought to shake off the violence that had surfaced, the shocking anger that he felt, just briefly, for the woman he loved so dearly.

He was going out of his mind. She was right to be worried.

All he knew was that everything would be okay again, just as soon as he got to Wansham. Once he was there, everything would become clear.

Martin Shackleford was almost sure he recognized the hysterical woman. He sat in the corner of the lounge bar of the Royal Oak hotel in Wansham and watched the two uniformed policemen trying to calm her down. She was making little sense, and her broken sobbing, and the noise of the television above the bar itself, made it difficult for Shackleford to fully grasp the reason for her distress.

He stared at her across the distance, trying to remember where and when he might have seen her before. At last the police escorted her from the hotel's lounge, and the landlord who had been standing solemn-faced and irritable, watching the proceedings, visibly relaxed.

The lounge was hardly crowded—a few weary-looking locals, and a plump, young London girl, busy making suggestive conversation with a youth from the village—but the landlord clearly liked his bar to be quiet, subdued, orderly.

Shackleford rose from his table, swirling the last of his beer in the bottom of the glass and draining it. He went to the bar and ordered a fresh pint. The landlord was a lot happier now. He was a ruddy-faced man called Seb Quinn; his white hair, wide moustaches, and portly build almost gave him the look of a caricature British publican. He loved a chat, and Shackleford had spent many an hour during the last summer, when he had stayed at this same, small hotel, chatting about nothing in particular with the man, and enjoying every minute of it.

"Husband's got lost," Quinn said, and smiled. "Can't say as I blame him." The landlord's accent was rustic, but not local.

"I've seen her before," said Shackleford, pulling up a bar stool. He paid for his pint, sipped the beer, and glanced towards the door where the police had taken her. "Was she here last summer?"

The landlord nodded. "That's right. Stayed here too, I remember. Her, her husband, and their scruffy son. You were here at the same time. What's going on, then?" He smiled. "Holiday reunion?"

"Felt like coming back," said Shackleford. "I enjoyed myself last year. Came back on a whim. The best way to take a holiday."

"Aye," said Quinn agreeably, then smiled, "mind you, it's not been so nice here this last couple of days." When Shackleford questioned him with a glance, he nodded at the door. "The couple, the lady there . . . arguing fit to kill. She didn't want to be back here no more than fly. He liked the place, insisted on coming for a week. I don't think they said one civil word to each other from the day they arrived."

"So he's walked off, you think?"

Seb Quinn chuckled. "Wouldn't have blamed him at all. Long as my bill gets paid. Went out yesterday, up to the seabluff and across the flats—" he meant the coastal pathway and the shore—"bloody bitter day, much as it's been today. And tomorrow too, no doubt. After a while she comes back in the car, red-faced, furious. Three double vodkas and not a nice word to say to a soul. But he doesn't turn up again, and she goes to bed alone. This morning she goes out looking for him, and now . . . well, if he's any sense he's home and dry in bed in Liverpool."

Mention of the "flats," the sand flats that served as a beach along the coast, sent a shiver down Shackleford's spine. There was something compellingly fascinating about that part of the town. It was the reason he had come back here, to walk along the trackways, up towards the sea, and feel the sea wind on his face, listen to the restless tides . . .

He'd arrived quite late, car trouble having held him up at Cambridge for a while. He had been inclined, at first, to go for a walk in the dusk, ignoring the rain, walking up to the sea just to remember. He had changed his mind at the thought of a good hot meal and a couple of pints, deciding to begin his tour tomorrow.

But the glimpse of the woman, and the chat about the bluff and the sea-flats, and the images that they had evoked in him, made him change his mind again. It was only six in the evening, and although the day was gone, it was still bright enough to see outside, and a brisk, swift walk to the sea and back would do him good.

What a pity, he thought, that Sharon couldn't be with me to share this treat. She really would have loved coming back.

The atmosphere of the place was so nice . . . it touched something deep inside him, made him feel almost at home. He belonged here, among the sleepy populace, propping up the bar of this small and cosy little pub, taking long walks out across the farmland, and along the bluffs of land where ridge-paths had been trodden for centuries.

"Think I'll take a walk," he said, draining his glass a little too fast, and feeling the warm beer bubble and froth in his stomach.

"Bit blowy," warned Quinn. "Rain forecast for later on again."

"Don't mind rain," said Shackleford, imitating the landlord's accent and smiling to show that he meant no offense.

"You ought to walk up to Oldun Ridge tomorrow. Digging up the old town, they are. The Roozie. Thousand years old, all the old timbers, holes in the ground, dustbin pits. Experts, four of them, up from London. She's one . . ." he nodded towards the adolescent girl in the corner, and scowled. "Still, that ought to bring the tourists out in force, come the summer."

Quinn was clearly pleased at the thought of extra profits. Shackleford had seen the enclosures, the tents, and the activity up on the ridge, as he had driven into town. He had been intrigued. Now he felt irritated. Wansham was nice enough without visitors in abundance. Why spoil it?

"I might well do that," he said as he left the bar, buttoning up his rain coat, and winding a thick scarf around his neck.

He walked easily through the small town—some people called Wansham a village, some a town, he had noticed, but to him, a village was a hamlet, and Wansham seemed much larger than that—past the shops, the other public house, the garage, and out towards the town's edge. At one point a landrover roared past from the coast road. It stopped outside his own hotel and two men got out, spoke briefly as the vehicle drove away, and then separated. One of them used a walking stick and the sound of it on the pavement was quite loud in the windy evening. Shackleford remarked all this only because the vehicle had been so unpleasantly loud, and had been driven— by a hard-faced young man, he thought—with such reckless speed. He guessed that they were the other three of the four "up from London," and digging around on the ridge at the site of the old settlement.

Just past the last house in Wansham, and standing on a rise of ground, was the church of St. Magnus, surrounded on four sides by its cemetery. Shackleford knew that he could reach the sea quickest by cutting through the churchyard, and he strode slowly round the sombre grey walls of the building, and towards the stile at the far side of the churchyard. There must have been a good moon up, because the clouds ahead of him, out across the sea, were brightly streaked as they moved rapidly across the dusk sky.

As he clambered across the stile, picking his footing carefully, he realized that the man with the stick was just entering the churchyard from the main road behind him, walking in the same direction. He hesitated, wondering whether to make polite conversation with a man who may have been planning the same brisk stroll to the sea, but decided against it. He wanted nothing to do with archaeologists.

But as he straightened and began to walk along the muddy pathway, the man called to him, "Glad you could make it."

Shackleford turned in surprise, but in the instant of turning, all confusion drained away, replaced by a wonderful sense of understanding and recognition. He even smiled, and although a part of him wondered at what was happening, he clambered back across into the graveyard, and called out, "I'm Martin Shackleford."

"Glad to see you, Mister Shackleford."

"I know you, don't I?" He walked towards the other man, torn between certainty and uncertainty, his limbs moving almost by their own volition.

"I'm the one who called you, Mister Shackleford. In that way, yes, you know me. We'll use the crypt, I think . . ."

Leaning on his stick, the stranger was reaching down and tugging at the wooden cover of the external stairs to the church's crypt. Shackleford couldn't see his face, but he knew that this man was quite old. He was well-spoken, almost arrogant in his tone of voice.

The man had opened the wooden cover and stepped down and out of sight. By the time Shackleford reached the steep, musty-smelling steps, there was a dim illumination rising from the stone-lined vault below. He could hear the sound of the stick as the man walked about.

Stepping carefully on the worn stone steps, Shackleford descended below the church. The crypt was quite small, dominated by four central stone tombs, its walls lined with shelves on which skulls were racked in their hundreds, most of them just the cranial boxes, missing the lower jaws. At the far side of the vault was a great mass of concrete, in which limb bones had been pressed, a strange and eerie monument to the dead.

"Where are you?"

"I'm here, Mister Shackleford."

Shackleford saw the old man, standing in a shadowy recess at the side of the crypt. The light came from a single battery-operated lamp, which had been positioned so that its light fell upon Shackleford; he could hardly make out the details of the old man's face, but he was sure that he was smiling.

"Amazing crypt, is it not?" said the cultured voice, and Shackleford glanced around, nodding. He was cold. The vault was heavy with the smell of stone, dust and damp.

"Wouldn't like to get stuck down here, that's for sure," he said, with a nervous laugh.

The man in the shadows laughed too. "Too late for that, Mister Shackleford . . ." and surprisingly, as he said it, Shackleford felt no more than a sense of acceptance . . . even though part of him twisted with horror, recognized that he was in deadly danger, desperately tried to scream out, and move the complacent body away from this sinister presence in the vault with him.

The man said, "These skulls are very old. Most of them are from a cemetery that was built nearby more than a thousand years ago. The skulls of Angles . . . you might prefer to think of them as Saxons, a more familiar name . . . and a few, I can see, are of the Nordic peoples. The vikings. See how many of them have holes in them. Weapons, Mister Shackleford; knives, arrows, swords, axes. Especially axes. There were battles fought here, and roundabouts, throughout all that long period of the first millennium. They buried their dead, and we unburied them and stored them here. Perhaps a few of these fine grinning specimens once walked within the palisade of the Oldun Ridge settlement."

He stopped speaking. Shackleford stared at him, and wanted to converse with him as one man to another, ordinary things, questions, greetings; anything. Anything normal.

But it was not normal. He couldn't move his jaws. He couldn't get his thoughts straight. What the hell was he doing here? What on earth had prompted him to come back to the town . . . ?

And yet he knew what it was. It was coming home. It was answering the call. It was returning. It was bringing back what belonged to the other man.

Arm raised above his head, the old man stepped quickly out from the shadows; but it was no longer a human shape that stood there. The smiling face had become a screaming skull, lank, fair hair hanging from the tatters of flesh that remained on the bone. It moved rapidly towards Shackleford, who screeched with terror and fell back against the shelves of bones, trying to avert his eyes from the shimmering grey horror that loomed before him.

He saw the glint of light on a metal-bladed axe, and heard the air parted with that swishing sound that means the passage of a cutting edge. The axe came down towards him, but he flung himself to one side and heard skulls shattered, felt and saw shards of ancient white bone fly onto the ground before him. He stumbled as he ran around the vault, and as he frantically pulled himself upright, hanging onto the edge of one of the stone coffins, the axe struck through his fingers, and glanced off the stone, embedding itself between his parted teeth as he screamed in pain.

He was still alive, but only just, as the axe blade was worked free from the sinew and bone that snagged it.

—FOUR

ANGELA HUXLEY WATCHED fascinated from the French window as Dan Brady made a breach in the psychic defences around his house. He freely admitted that his technique was probably crude and unnecessarily damaging, but without Ellen Bancroft to advise him, for the moment he had to depend on intuition.

He cut several channels through the line of earth mazes, using an iron knife. He moved the braziers on that side of the house, and hoped that the wind would soon disperse the invisible aromatic screen of incense from the mandrake and other herbal mix that formed the *zona mandragora*. He then dug up four of the clay gargoyles from their embedded positions below the lawns and garden.

He was now quite vulnerable to elemental attack. Angela Huxley could tell that for certain because, to her delight and great comfort, she was suddenly reunited with the cacophonic sound of the world Beyond.

Until Brady had destroyed that last zone, she had stood watching with the uncanny void of silence a distracting and unusual presence in her mind; she was quite unfamiliar with being left alone so completely with her thoughts. She had noticed a strange ringing tone. She had been aware of growing more edgy, not with Brady or Andrew Haddingham, but with herself, thoughts and considerations tumbling naked and harsh in her clear-headed state. She had seemed to be more exposed to her own mind than in all the rest of her adult life.

Then Brady had broken the *zona magnetica*. Immediately she had become aware of a sound like rushing wind; the whispering had grown louder as the gargoyles had emerged from the earth, and soon she could distinguish individual whispers, the moans, the cries, the shouts, the incoherent mumblings of the spiritual essences that crowded the various planes, or corridors, of the Hinterland, corridors that led from each to that final, silent peace.

When the zones were fully breached, the roar of the spirit world in her mind was complete, and her body relaxed, the shaking in her hands went away. It was an uncanny and welcome experience to be so aware, even if only briefly, of the quality of that presence in her mind. She had become so used to it that she ignored it. She had forgotten the components of distress and anguish that added to the softer, more contented murmuring of spirits moving onwards.

Within minutes, as she sat down in an armchair and composed herself, the noise, the intense whispering, was something she had to work hard to acknowledge. Perhaps an ordinary man, presented with this otherworldly sound, would have run screaming from the room, beating his head, desperately trying to shake some clarity into his mind. But Angela was used to the noise, it was a part of her, and she could no more function without it than she could function in the absence of a demonstrable heartbeat.

It was nearly four in the afternoon. The brief flurry of rain had stopped. The lights in the lounge were on because of the overcast day, and the gloomy storm-clouds building towards evening.

And she could immediately feel the disturbance in the Hinterland.

It was something she had noticed, vaguely, that morning. There had been a violent entry to the Hinterland, a violent arrival. It had quickly become swamped by the noise, and she had remarked it only slightly; the arrival had probably been sometime during the preceding day, but she had slept more than twenty hours before coming to Brook's Corner, after a long seance session in Bristol, and had probably not been aware of the *precise* moment of arrival.

But the feel of the spirit, the experience of it, left her in no doubt at all: someone had been killed in the last twenty-four hours, violently killed, and the spirit was clinging desperately to the corpse, unwilling to let go fully. A strange, eerie and very discomforting thought. And quite irrelevant to the matters at hand.

Brady sat down opposite her, sweating slightly from the exertion of digging. His hands were filthy, but he had decided not to wash them; his jeans were grimy from kneeling on the muddy ground. He looked wild and dishevelled, but he gave Angela a quick, cheering smile, then said, "What can you feel?"

"You mean what can I hear? It's back again, the sound of the Hinterland. A very comforting presence, Mister Brady." She smiled.

Andrew Haddingham asked, "Why don't you call it the Astral Plane?"

"Because it's not the Astral Plane," she replied simply. "I'm sensitive to the corridors that lead to that plane, if indeed it exists. The spirit, as it travels onwards, takes many and various routes, some of which bring it quite close to earth again. The closest of these is the Hinterland; the furthest is what I call the Shoreline, a bright, breezy place, rather like the seaside. When a spirit passes beyond the Shoreline, I find it almost impossible to call it back. Some spirits are in the Hinterland still, even though they arrived centuries ago. They become fossilized. I call them Stonefaces. They can acknowledge me, but we don't communicate..." she stopped talking, glanced at Brady, who was regarding her thoughtfully. "So tell me what it is you'd like me to do."

"Twice before," said Brady, leaning forward slightly, "you've brought me a message from the Hinterland."

"*I* have?" She was confused. She was sure that this was the first time she had met Dan Brady. What was he talking about? "I'm sure you're wrong..."

"I wasn't at the seance where it happened. I wasn't present. But you had observers from the Ennean Institute in the room..."

That wasn't surprising. She worked quite closely with several centres of Paranormal Research. She asked, "Were you among them?"

"As I said, I wasn't there. I worked at Hillingvale, with Andrew here. But in the accounts of your seance contacts you twice received a garbled, peculiar message from an unidentified source. The message was simple: *Tell Dan that they are Awakening. Tell Dan that they are reaching.* That's all. But it came twice. I didn't think until recently that the message was intended for me, but now I'm sure of it."

Angela struggled to remember the occasions. She was well used to spirit contacts emerging from the strange fog of the Hinterland, speaking briefly, then retiring without identifying themselves, and without indicating to whom they wished to speak; but invariably *someone* present knew the source, recognized the content. A seance was a communal mind, where Angela became the channel for the feeble thought-contact of those present for the stronger spiritual presence of those in the Hinterland with whom they had rapport. It was unheard-of for a message to be addressed to someone not present . . .

And even as she thought through her own experience as a medium, so she remembered . . .

"The weeping man!" she said. And even as she said it she was thinking no, it's not possible. Surely! The weeping man, a Stoneface, who she had thought was doing no more than struggle to communicate. A silent, ancient presence in the Hinterland. Had he in fact managed to send a message through?

Brady was perplexed, shaking his head as he asked, "Who's the weeping man?"

"A fossilized spirit. One of the Stonefaces." Angela looked deeply thoughtful. "He's present in the Hinterland, and I think I've been aware of him for all my adult life. I think of him as weeping, but that's just the sense I get of him; a man betrayed, and irreconcilably sorrowed by the fact. I often dream about the Hinterland, and whenever I glimpse him he looks as if he's weeping . . ."

"Does he address you? Does he talk through you?"

She looked uncertain. "I know he's tried. I'm sure of that. But I didn't think he'd succeeded. But suddenly, as you tell me what that message contained, I've started to be aware of him again . . ."

Haddingham asked, "Are you always aware of the spirit communication that occurs through you?"

His question dragged her back from her thoughts. She nodded. "I always have *some* recollection. Or at least, I'd thought that was the case. May I see the transcripts of the contact? Do you have them?"

Brady went to the bureau and fetched out several sheets of typed paper. As she read down the question and answer sequence she realized that this meant nothing to her; she had no recollection at all of any such contact. She might have been reading someone else's seance:

Who can I tell?
Q. Who are you?
Who can I tell?
Q. What do you wish to tell?
Who can I tell?
Q. Will you identify yourself. Do you have a name?
Who can I tell?
Q. What do you wish to tell?
They are awakening.
Q. Who is awakening?
They can reach. They have reached. They are awakening.
Q. Who is this message for? Is it for anyone at this table?
Tell him. Tell him they are awakening. Tell Dan. Tell him.
Q. Who is Dan?
Tell Dan. They are gathering. They have reached.

The report ended with the blunt comment: *AH emerges from trance and is physically sick. Reports that she felt as if she had been in an ice-cold wind.*

"I remember *that*!" she said. "But none of this . . ." she was astonished to read the words, and to have no recollection at all of the contact. "I remember being sick, but I'd thought it was a difficult contact. Nobody said anything to me. I went on and contacted someone else . . ."

But, of course, the observers from the Ennean Institute had documented that brief communication, thinking as little of it as the rest of those who sat around the table, those who were eager for words from dead relatives, messages from beyond.

"If I'd known . . ." she said, and the image—part sound, part vision—of the weeping man, the age-old Stoneface lurking in the recesses of the Hinterland, was powerful. It had *had* to be him. Something in that brief, difficult contact had blocked her memory of the content. Twice.

"Do you want me to try for him again?" she asked.

"Yes," said Brady. "Please. Tell him that Dan is here. Ask him to repeat the message."

"*You* must ask that. I'm not promising that I can even make the contact. It's usually they who contact me responding to the minds around me. Keep your fingers crossed..."

They pulled the curtains and turned out the main lights in the lounge, using two corner lamps which cast a cosy glow across the room. "Try to keep your minds concentrated on me, and the idea of contact," she said, closing her eyes and relaxing. She immediately experienced the dull colours of the Hinterland, the shifting forms, the dark areas, the patchy areas of light, and the eerie sensation of being watched.

"Dan is here," she said, and searched among the visual images for a glimpse of the Stoneface. "Dan is here," she repeated, and let the word, "Awakening," sit in her consciousness, intuiting that this word might be a trigger for the ancient spiritual contact.

Several spirit-forms pushed forward and tried to speak. One she recognized, a gabbling life-form that had been fifty or sixty years in the Hinterland and which seemed urgent just to *talk*. She discouraged her and the gabbler drew back, sulking (or at least, that was Angela's experience of the withdrawal of a spirit not called upon). There was a young girl whose presence was like a bird, darting back and forth, unseen, heard only by the voice, which was frail, uncertain, terribly lost. Because it was important to her, Angela let the voice grow stronger, encouraged the girl to speak, for a moment, and she heard the name "Mai-li."

"Do you know a girl called Mai-li? She's Chinese. She died recently, violently, I think."

Brady said (astonished), "Yes. Yes, I do. She was a nurse on my ward when I was in hospital. She was killed..." he didn't add that she had been killed by a projection of psychic evil that had been trying to get to him as he had lain helpless in bed, recovering from his wounds.

Angela said, "She is very frightened."

Brady asked, "Can I help her in any way?"

But all Angela could get from the restless spirit of the girl was the question, "Why? Why?" The girl was desperately unhappy. It might be some time before she found peace, before she could journey beyond the Shoreline.

And as abruptly as she had come forward, the darting spirit withdrew among the Shades.

Angela Huxley grew weary. It was a very tiring process, concentrating so hard on summoning a particular Shade. And the spirit that she sought was at the best of times almost totally reluctant to communicate.

It was after six in the evening before she began to discern some auditory hint of the Stoneface—a deeper, more mellow voice than usual, a whispered contact from among the murmuring of the thousands. All she discerned with her mind's eye was a hardening of a part of the flowing darkness, the hint of a shape, keeping its distance.

Brady had been growing weary too. He watched Angela Huxley tiredly, stifling the yawn that came on, beginning to accept that he would fail, today at least, to get a clue as to where to take his search. Haddingham had been dozing lightly, on and off, and Brady wondered whether or not his lack of attention had been contributing to the medium's failure to draw the Stoneface out of its hidey-hole.

He felt restless, edgy. He couldn't get thoughts of Alison out of his mind, even though he usually managed to control his feelings of loneliness well; it was the weariness of the body, and the slowness of the evening, making him dream of her, bringing her forward, like his own particularly harrowing Shade, haunting him.

He was deeply glad that Angela had detected no sign of her, or the children, in the crowded realm of the Hinterland.

He noticed the sudden tension in Angela, and sat up a little straighter. Her face, its eyes still closed, creased into a deep frown, the lines around her eyes and across her forehead deepening, then vanishing as—within her skull—some scene, some act of contact was played out.

"Dan is here," she whispered, repeating the phrase, then uttering what could only be described as a slightly strangled cry.

She said, "They are awakening." Her voice was strange. It

was undeniably hers, but its quality was subtly altered, a deeper tone, with a disembodied feel to it. "They are awakening, awakening. Reaching, awakening."

Brady said, "Will you identify yourself? Who are you?"

The spirit replied, "No name. There is no name. For me. No name. They came from the sea. Betrayed. Betrayed. The youth with the voice of friendship. No name. No name. I am the walker in shadow. No name. Tell Dan. Tell Dan ..."

"I am Dan," said Brady loudly, ernestly, watching Angela's face as it grimaced and twisted, almost as if in pain. "My name is Daniel Brady. I am the one to whom you wish to speak."

There was an agonizing silence. Angela's head turned from side to side very slowly. Brady noticed that her fingers gripped the arms of her chair with incredible strength, the fabric pulled in almost to the wooden frame; the tendons stood out on the backs of her hands, and on her neck. Was she in pain?

"You are the one," she said, speaking with the voice of the dead.

Again silence. Brady prompted, "I am the one for what? What can I do? Where do I go? You must help me."

"The Talisman," came the words. "The stone of power. It lies below the lodge. They must not find it."

"What Talisman? Where do I go?"

"They are close to the sea," came the deep voice from Angela Huxley's dry lips. She seemed to become agitated. "They are with the one who was betrayed."

Exasperated, Brady urged, "Which sea? Where by the sea? You *must* tell me ..."

"In the place of Uffric's people. The dead! The dead!"

Brady was about to question further, but he realized that all was not well with the woman who sat so restlessly before him. The movement of her head had become faster, more erratic. There was a thin stream of spittle on her chin, her mouth gaping more. Her eyes were clenched tight shut, and her body fidgeted and twisted, as if she were being tortured. Haddingham rose from his chair and went to her, reaching towards her in an attempt to wake her, and calm her down.

Suddenly, shockingly, she began to scream, making the older man back away from her.

She had sat bolt upright in the chair, hands on the arms, body rigid. Her eyes were wide, staring ahead of her, at Brady, directed at Brady. The scream persisted, her mouth widening, saliva flowing down her chin. Her face became suffused with blood, and then abruptly became white as the paper on which Brady had been writing.

It was a frightening transfiguration. The flesh on her face was unnaturally pale, and her eyes seemed to sink, her lips draw back, her head cock to one side...

It was a screaming skull, the bone poking through thin, tattered flesh, the mouth wide and agonized, the dead eyes staring blindly.

It was a face he recognized well, for he had drawn it for the police only a few weeks ago, in hospital as he recovered from the attack on him.

The face of an amulet, a screaming head, carved in stone, and worn around the neck of a man, dressed all in black, who had bent towards him and discovered him to be still alive...

What do we do?
He's not wanted. Kill him. Quickly.
That's forbidden for me.
Then bring the fetch...

And while they had spoken above his broken body, Alison and Marianna and shy Dominick had been carried from the darkened lounge, unconscious figures, slung across the shoulders of the men who had come out of the night.

Arachne.

The Collectors. Taking his family into the darkness, taking them away from him, inexplicably, totally. Leaving him for dead...

He fought down his fear as he stared at the shimmering, screaming face before him, half aware that he was seeing some terrible manifestation from what Angela Huxley called the Hinterland.

A moment later the apparition was gone, and the woman slumped heavily back into her seat, head lolling, eyes half closed. Her desperate grip on the arms of the chair relaxed.

Both Brady and Haddingham ran to her, patting her hands, moving her face, trying to bring her back from whatever state of unconsciousness she had descended into.

A minute or so later her eyes grew bright, alert. She straightened slightly, started to shake. Looking directly at Brady, she said, "My God, what happened?"

"Your face . . ." he said. "It transformed. Like a skull. A mask. A screaming mask."

She looked away from him, nodding slightly. "An arrival. A violent arrival. Terrified. It came into the Hinterland and latched upon me, struggling to return. Nothing like that has ever happened to me before . . ."

Haddingham was astonished. "A murdered man? Is that what you mean? Someone murdered at this *very moment*?"

Angela turned hollow eyes upon him. "Yes. Seconds ago . . ." she sounded weak, shaken. "He's terrified. I can still . . . I can still hear him screaming, very lost, very confused . . ." She looked at Brady, shaking her head. "I'm not sure, but I think there's a connection with the Stoneface. Whoever just died seemed to . . . seemed to *recognize* me through the Stoneface . . ."

Brady said, "Contact him. Call the dead man up. If that's true, he can tell us *where* he died. Perhaps that's where . . ." he broke off. Wild thinking, confused thinking. But it was a hope, a straw to clutch, that the "new" arrival had been dispatched by Arachne as the Collectors journeyed north. He needed something, *anything*, to give him an idea of where to start to look . . .

Angela Huxley was saying, "I can't contact him. I don't dare." Her voice was almost a whisper, and she sat back and touched hands to her face, feeling how cold and clammy her flesh had become. "I'm very tired, now. It will take some time for him to settle—yes, I believe, it's a man who just died. The same as yesterday . . ."

"Yesterday?" prompted Brady.

"There was a violent arrival yesterday as well. I was asleep at the time, but when I woke I could sense him there."

"Same violence?"

"I think so. I'm only aware of a very few arrivals." She smiled quickly, glancing at Brady. "I'd go mad if that weren't the case, I expect."

Brady said, "You don't get overloaded during war-time, then."

Angela shook her head thoughtfully. "I have no real idea what governs my particular awareness. Geographic spread? Perhaps. Perhaps deaths that can sense an association, through me, with earthly forces that are important to them. I'm aware of a great many deaths, but few of them affect me the way that that last arrival affected me. When someone who has been unnaturally killed arrives in the Hinterland there is always a long period of settling. Rather like your Ellen, although her difficulties were compounded. Perhaps if we tried in a few days we might get a contact with one of the dead..."

"Perhaps," said Brady. He stood up straight, peering down at the woman. "Is the Stoneface still there?"

She shook her head. "I'm too tired anyway, Mister Brady. What happened to me then was... unnerving." She glanced up. "I transformed? My face changed...?"

Haddingham reassured her. "Not literally. An apparition, a spectral face, appeared around you, superimposed upon you."

Brady said, "I've seen that face before. Not as a ghost, not as an apparition, but on an amulet." Angela regarded him blankly, then frowned slightly. Brady went on, "One of the men that night who tried to kill me was wearing a stone amulet. I can still see him, leaning down towards me, and the screaming skull dangling before my face..."

Angela murmured, "Then there *is* a connection. Between my Stoneface, the murdered man... this amulet and the people who took your family..."

Haddingham said, "The Stoneface, speaking through you, referred to a talisman. 'They must not find it.' A stone of power, it said. Perhaps talisman and amulet are one and the same."

"Or the amulet that *I* saw a copy of the stone carving they are seeking," said Brady softly. "The sea," he went on, and laughed, more with irony than with humour. "A place by the sea called the place of Uffric's people. Oh, and it has a ridge. How long is the coastline of Britain, I wonder?"

Haddingham smiled too. "It's not enough, is it. We *could* call the British Museum. It's possible that Uffric's town has been excavated at some time..."

"Would you do that for me?" said Brady gently. "I don't think I could cope with sitting in a library for several weeks, leafing through old journals."

"I can certainly ask," said Haddingham warily.

Angela Huxley stood up and pulled on her coat, buttoning it up with hands that shook badly. "I must go. It's been quite an experience, Mister Brady. I wish you every success, and please call on me, and on my services, at any time you might need me. I shall always be available."

"Thank you for all your help. I appreciate it very much."

Andrew Haddingham drove the woman home.

A thought had occurred to Brady on which he now pinned all his hopes of being able to commence a more determined search for his family. If a man *had* been killed sometime, late the previous day, then there was a chance of a small report appearing in one of the larger papers the following morning. It was equally possible that a report of the death that had occurred just minutes before might appear, but Brady felt it was rather late in the evening to make the news—and there was always the thought that the body might not be found for some time.

He rose at five, as usual, having spent a sleepless night remembering the eerie words of the fossil Shade from the Hinterland, and trying to force an image of Alison and his two children being trudged northwards during the dark, damp nights, prisoners of evil, their time rapidly running out. He walked quickly around the garden, checking his re-built defences, then jogged to the local shops and was there when the papers were delivered. He fetched back a copy of every paper and returned with them to the lounge of Brook's Corner, where he made a pot of strong coffee and sat down at the table.

He studied every column in intricate detail, searching for some hint of a killing, the first confused reports of a murder. It might be no more than a tiny mention on the inner pages, but something inside him, some intuition, had convinced him that a report *would* be carried.

In the event, by ten o'clock, when he had scoured and double-scoured all eight papers, he had come up with nothing.

He rose wearily from the dining table and walked across the lounge towards the hallway. He needed more coffee, and something to eat. He was dizzy with concentration.

The lounge door slammed shut before him.

Brady spun round in sudden shock, his immediate thought being that he was coming under psychic attack . . . that he had failed to rebuild the defences correctly.

Wind blew down the chimney and a grey flurry of dead ash gusted out into the room. The curtains, still drawn across the room's windows, flapped wildly, as if blown by a gale.

Calming down fast, more puzzled, now, than panicked, Brady stood by the door and watched the poltergeist activity around him.

The papers on the table rustled and were thrown and scattered about the floor. Only one remained on the table. Its sheets were turned by unseen fingers, and then that too was sent flying across the room; it landed, a crumpled heap at his feet, and he bent to pick it up.

Again, then, he leafed through the *Daily Telegraph*, scanning each column carefully.

And he found it, and had missed it only because he had been looking for the report of a murder.

Delighted with himself, and loudly acknowledging the ghostly irritation of Ellen Bancroft, he spread the relevant page out on the table and read through the brief report several times. Headlined, MISSING BUSINESSMAN, it recorded only that businessman John Keeton had gone missing whilst on holiday in East Anglia, close to the tiny fenland-edge village of Wansham. The police were concerned that Mister Keeton might have suffered a memory lapse and have wandered south, or caught a train or bus, or hitched a lift out of the area. His behaviour, for some days, had not been that of a totally rational man.

John Keeton.

The first arrival.

"Sorry Mrs. Keeton," said Brady to the newspaper column. "But your man's a lot further away than you think."

Another consideration was exciting him too. Wansham—when he checked his road map—turned out to be only thirty miles from another village he had recently visited: Medfield, where the late George Campbell, Superintendent of the Ministry of Defence Station at Hillingvale, had his large, country home.

George Campbell . . . the mind behind the psychic attacks that had claimed Ellen Bancroft's life, and nearly claimed Brady's own.

Two villages, connected with the force of evil that he called Arachne, and only thirty miles apart. It was an area, then, of great interest to Brady.

The real hunt was beginning at last.

Five

KETT'S FARM WAS a smallholding of thirty acres, tucked in between the sea and the crest of land known as Oldun Ridge, where the excavations were taking place in these mid-Spring months. The farm could scarcely cut a profit, so many of those thirty acres being bad grazing land, waterlogged marsh and, something that was a rarity in this part of the world, over five acres of peat bogland, part of a swathe of peat that stretched as far as Little Minster, ten miles away.

Jack and Karen Seymour arrived in Wansham shortly after midday, after a fast, reckless drive north in their hired car. Karen took one look at the drab farmhouse, and the dreary, ramshackle out-buildings of the farm, and her depression was confirmed.

It had been bad enough in summer, when the yard had been dry and there had been a cheery sun to give the landscape a sleepy, idyllic quality; in this wet, overcast Spring, the fields looked bleak and uninviting, the farm building almost uninhabitable.

"Oh God, I don't think I can face this . . ."

"You'll enjoy yourself!" Jack said it almost as an order. He swung the car through the opened gates and sounded the horn twice. Chickens scattered before them as they drove round to the front of the main farmhouse. Karen sank down in her seat, her mood of gloom deepening. "Greasy bacon. Freezing rooms. Spiders in the bath. Soggy walks up to our knees in mud. Jack! Let's go somewhere else!"

Jack Seymour said nothing. He looked coldly angry, tired of his wife's constant disgruntlement. He stepped from the car and walked up to the house, where he met Agnes Hadlee, the plump and jolly woman who ran the household side of Kett's Farm. Karen watched from the warmth of the car, smiled thinly at the woman when she waved at her, and prayed that the Hadlees had suffered a family bereavement and could not, now, take them in.

Up on the ridge, Karen noticed, several figures moved slowly about between canvas tents. They looked as if they were digging. As she stared at them she caught the glint of sparse sunlight on binoculars, and realized that one of the distant figures was watching her.

It made her shiver slightly. It was unnerving to feel that she was being coldly regarded from across a quarter of a mile. But she put it down to the man's curiosity . . . perhaps Farmer Hadlee himself, seeing if it was his guests who had turned up.

Jack came back to the car and unlocked the boot, where the cases were stowed. "Are you coming?" he called, and Karen reluctantly stepped out into the cold, brisk day. Wrapping her coat around her she trod warily, and unhappily, to the farmhouse, greeted Mrs. Hadlee as pleasantly as she could, and then followed her up the creaking stairway to the damp, musty guest room, with its grim view over the fields and the distant pathway to the sea.

We could at least have stayed in the town's hotel! But not Jack. On no. It had to be exactly as it was before . . .

She unpacked slowly, feeling almost reluctant to expose her clothes to the atmosphere in the room. Jack washed briskly, and changed into his old jeans and jumper. Then, without a word to Karen, he trotted down the stairs and out of the house, walking along the edge of one of the fields towards the sea. Karen watched him from the window, distressed and close to tears.

What was happening to him? What was happening to *them*? She was unused to such abrupt coldness, the turning off of his compassion and caring for her. Perhaps he was angry with her for not sharing his appreciation of his mad ideas, but normally he would have shown *some* sensitivity towards her.

Dammit, she was four months pregnant! She *needed* a bit of support at this time!

When she had unpacked, and had told herself off for her maudlin self-pity, she went down to the kitchen for a cup of coffee with Agnes Hadlee. She tried to be cheerful, but she was distracted by thoughts of Jack. The woman noticed, and seemed to understand that all was not well with her guest. She made cheerful bantering conversation, fussing around the kitchen as she prepared sandwiches and rolls.

"Pity the weather's so dull for you. This part of the country can be really very nice in Spring. Long way to come for so much cold and rain."

Karen sipped her coffee, then said, "To be honest with you, and please don't take offence . . . but I didn't want to come at all. It was Jack who wanted to see the place again."

Agnes Hadlee brought over a plate of sandwiches, and sat down at the scratched and unpolished pine table. "Is that right? I thought it was odd that a young couple like you would want to come back to a place like this twice in a year. Didn't like to say anything . . ." She gave such a sweet smile that Karen relaxed instantly, leaning her elbows on the table as she cradled the warm cup.

"He's going through something, Mrs. Hadlee. I don't understand it, I certainly don't like it. But what can I do? I've never known him so determined to do something so . . . well, crazy. His behaviour is crazy!"

"Very odd," she agreed, then frowned. "Very odd indeed."

"Why do you say that?" Mrs. Hadlee had been referring to something *other* than Jack's behaviour, Karen had guessed.

The older woman looked up, then shrugged slightly. She was wondering whether to tell Karen something, and being an honest sort she was transparent in her uncertainty. Then she said, "There was another couple in the town. They came back too, after being here last summer."

"When?"

"Well, just the other day. Older couple than you. There's been a lot of fuss about it."

"Fuss?"

"*He's* disappeared. Not her, just him. Local talk says there was a row, up on the sea bluff, and she walked off and left him. But he didn't come back that evening. The police are still in the town, asking questions, looking around. Reporter from one of the papers too. Quite a fuss."

Karen was silent for a moment, feeling chilled, almost frightened. She was remembering what Jack had said, a few days ago: *It's a feeling, a terrible irresistible feeling that someone wants to speak to me. Perhaps I met someone last time we were there* . . .

"What happened to him, do you think?"

Mrs. Hadlee shook her head and smiled. "Anybody's guess. And most people are guessing that he's a hundred miles away, starting a new life. Not the happiest of couples, if you'll forgive me passing judgement on strangers."

"It's not really likely, though, is it?" said Karen with a weak smile. "Deserting your wife on the coast of Norfolk?"

"Not really. You're right. Myself, I think he's a hundred feet down, rather than a hundred miles away."

"Sucked into a bog, you mean."

"It's so treacherous out along the bluff, just on this side. The land is so wet, you see, and with all the rain we've had . . . There're parts along the edge of our land too which are fenced off. We lose animals there all the time. I remember what happened to your husband last year—he had a bit of a close shave, didn't he?"

"Yes. He did. He was lucky there was someone around to help him out." The two women regarded each other in silence for a moment. Karen said, "So you think a bog got him, this other man . . ."

"I'm sure of it. But the fuss will last for a while. And then the police will go away, and there'll be one more ghost to haunt Wansham, as if we didn't have enough already."

Karen was thinking of Jack, walking alone, out towards the ocean. "I'm glad there aren't *two* more ghosts. Last summer Jack was very careless."

Agnes Hadlee could see Karen's concern, and she glanced through the kitchen window. "He'll be all right. I can see him. He's up on the bluff, watching the sea." She looked at Karen and gave her that reassuring smile again. "You're very troubled my dear, very troubled."

"Well, yes I am. What are we doing here? We bundled our son off to my sister's, we spent a fortune on the flight, we're putting our new baby at risk . . ." she touched her stomach delicately, "and it's all because of a whim of Jack's. I can't live without him, I *have* to support him. I'm terrified, Mrs. Hadlee. Terrified for his mind, for our marriage. This village is haunting him, possessing him. It's as if . . ."

"As if what, my dear? Don't be afraid to speak what's on your mind."

"It's as if he lost part of his niceness, a part of his personality when we were here before. Since we went back to Edmonton he's been edgy, short-tempered, increasingly distracted. It only started to really dawn on me when he began to talk of nothing else—and I mean *nothing* else—but our holiday here."

Mrs. Hadlee rose from the table and fetched the coffeepot, refilling Karen's cup, and remaining thoughtfully silent. Her round, happy face was unusually drawn, a touch tense at the edges of her mouth. She bustled about the kitchen, and Karen watched her uneasily. "What is it?" Karen asked finally.

Mrs. Hadlee stopped by the sink, not looking at the younger woman. "I don't know, my dear. It's what you said about your husband being haunted by this village." She shook her head slowly, staring out through the window. "It's a village with a history of tragedy, and haunting. There are ghosts here, some real, some just part of folklore, but a lot of them tell of all manner of unpleasantness. I've got used to it, in a way, but I remember when I first came here . . ." she paused.

"What about when you first came here?"

"I hated the place, the village, the farm. Everything. There's an atmosphere in the area, a haunted, frightened feel. Something had happened here once. A long time ago. A betrayal, they say. Men murdered in their beds at night. A very bad happening that has scarred the land ever since."

"And have you seen the ghosts?"

"I've seen all manner of things. Ghosts? Yes, a few. I've seen the running couple, young lovers, running out across the styke. To find a bit of peace and quiet no doubt. But I've also seen the screaming man. He haunts the Roozie, up on the ridge. Up there where they're working. Terrifying sight, a tall, half naked man, long hair, running through the night screaming. It's an evil apparition from an evil time..."

She turned and sat down at the table again. Karen half thought that this little tour of local legend was designed to take her mind off Jack, and her problems, but Agnes Hadlee's face was too serious, too concerned. She was speaking from the heart, with no cynicism at all. "I sometimes wonder," she said, "whether or not visitors become a part of that evil. I've had many people come and stay here, and they all feel it. It's an uncomfortable town. People *don't* usually come back, after they've visited. Not until these last few days, at least."

"What are you saying to me? That Jack may have been sensitive to a local feeling of fear, of despondency? That it may just be that the aura of the place has infected him?"

Mrs. Hadlee reached out and covered Karen's hand with her own. "It may be that simple," she said. "People and places have funny connections. Perhaps your husband has roots here. You're an English couple originally, aren't you?"

Karen shook her head. "Just Jack. His parents were English. His father was from Norfolk, which is why we came here last summer."

"Well there you are, then. I wouldn't worry about him, my dear. But we'll keep an eye on him for you."

Karen appreciated the older woman's care, even though the gesture was substantially empty. Changing the subject, she asked about the men working up on the ridge.

Agnes Hadlee sat back with an expression that told whole paragraphs about her disapproval. "If you ask me, they're the cause of the bad feeling at the moment. I've never known the ghosts of the village so active as since those people came."

"Are they excavating?"

"That they are. Down from London, four of them, one of them a sour-faced girl who spends most of her time in the local pubs, wishing she was somewhere else."

"Who are they?"

"As I say, they're archaeologists. They're digging up the old town. Saxon, they say. Thousands of years old, and best left undisturbed if you ask me. What on earth will they do with it once they've dug it up?"

"Cover it over again," said Karen with a smile. "That's the point of archaeology."

"Best left undisturbed. We always knew it was there. Locals—real locals, that is—call the place the Roozie—"

"Yes, I know."

"It's an old word, means 'bad luck.' Local couples walk four times round the Roozie before they get married. That way they ward off bad luck for the first seven years of their marriage. But since those four came down from London, the village has been very restless. I don't like them at all, though I don't mind selling them a few eggs and pints of milk. Every little helps."

"One of them was watching the farmhouse. Through binoculars."

Mrs. Hadlee wasn't surprised at all. "Probably the girl, looking to see if there's anyone arriving who looks more fun than the old men she works with. Darn nuisance, she is. Caused two ructions in the village, two engagements broken. Destructive little hussy. She's the daughter of Doctor Herbert, he's in charge up there . . ." she broke off as the sound of a landrover roared through the stillness outside. "Talk of the devil," she said with a wry smile at Karen. "More eggs, probably."

Karen followed her to the back door, and stood just inside, watching the two men who climbed out of the battered and muddy vehicle. They were both grey-haired and on the wrong side of fifty, she guessed, one of them smiling broadly—Agnes Hadlee murmured that this was Doctor Ewen Holbrook—the other a sour-faced, hard-eyed man, who leaned heavily on a stick. This was Doctor Herbert, the man in charge.

"Good afternoon," greeted the cheerful Holbrook. He glanced at Karen and gave her a half acknowledgement. The other man just stared, then turned and walked around the front of the house.

They'd had trouble with their generator, and wondered if James Hadlee could manage the loan of certain parts, just for two days or so. Mrs. Hadlee was sure that was possible. Her husband was at the market in Little Minster, at the moment, but she was sure it would be all right. They had an old generator which they weren't using.

As she and Doctor Holbrook disappeared towards one of the decaying barns that enclosed the quadrangle of the muddy yard, Karen stepped out of the house and walked to the gate, which overlooked the nearer field.

In the distance she could see Jack, a small, dark silhouette against the brightly clouded sky. He was running to and fro along the bluff like an excited child, seeking out to sea; searching.

The solemn man from the archaeological site was walking along the trackway towards him, leaning heavily on his stick, occasionally glancing back across his right shoulder, as if nervous about being followed.

It was an exhilarating feeling, running along the bluff, the seawind cold and fresh in his face, scented with weed and salt, a fine spray touching his skin like a sheen of dew. The land below him seemed to rock, to pitch and heave, the sea swelling around him, dark mountains of grey death, crashing across him, sweeping across the dark planks of some imagined ship.

Exhilaration. A sense of motion that made his mind whirl, his body sway as he paced this way, then that along the bluff, searching out to sea for the sail, for the black sail, for a sign of them.

In his mind there were obtrusive thoughts, which he resented, but was forced to acknowledge:

Mistake to bring Karen. Why in God's name did I ask her to come? Should have come alone. Don't need her. She's in the way, already in the way. She'll be hurt. Will have to hurt her. Mistake to insist she came, should have understood that better.

His body was physically exhausted. He was damp with sweat but he felt like laughing as he stood still, at last, and gulped breath into his lungs. The wind caught his hair, blew it back from his high forehead; it cooled his skin through his shirt, made him shiver with a sudden chill.

A day such as this, overcast, rainy. We met them on the shore, greeting them warmly. Murmurs of dissent among the others. Then the long walk back to the village; storm-whipped wraiths of smoke rising from beyond the walls . . .

Such strange thoughts. A part of him, yet not a part of him.

And still the sense of exhilaration.

Jack Seymour ran again, along the muddy path, towards a distance copse of trees, sheltered behind the bluff.

He felt a need to cry out, as if someone were whispering to him, urging him to rejoice. *I'm here, I'm back. I've come back. I'm here again* . . .

If the words did not emerge, the excitement was felt, nevertheless. It was a powerful sense of excitement, of returning, of belonging. Part of him questioned the experience. How could he feel so strongly about a place which he had visited on a brief holiday just eight months previous. He had felt very little, then, certainly not this overwhelming attachment to the bleak farmland, and the slushy, tree-lined hollows.

He had been here before and it had been longer ago than eight months. He had walked this landscape; he had surmounted this same bluff; the wind had been icy, gusting through his ragged, fur-lined clothes. He had led his friends between the bogs, and the scattered trees, along the cattle track towards the town on the ridge.

It had been a long time ago, a very long time ago. And yet the sensation of it was fresh, the differences between that day and this quite clear in his mind.

He glimpsed a man walking beyond the trees, and he scampered down the bluff, and picked his way carefully towards the shelter of that copse. He vaguely noticed that there was a fence around the hollow, marking off some particularly dangerous patch of bogland, no doubt. He walked swiftly towards it, calling out, "Hello! Hello there. It's Jack Seymour . . ."

Puzzlement. Why did I feel the need to say that? Who cares who I am?

He was answered by the wind in the swaying branches of the trees, the endless bubbling and gurgling of the ground, where water drained noisily. He glimpsed the man moving between the trunks and he changed direction, running slightly up the bluff so that he could work his way round and meet the stranger.

As he entered the dark confines of the copse, moving between the gnarled and clustered trees, he stumbled, sinking up to his knee in sticky, oily mud. "Damn!" he said, and looked up, realizing that the older man was close by to him, standing between two trees watching him. "I'm Jack Seymour. I'm back."

"So you are," said the man, and instantly Jack felt uneasy, glancing round at the unpleasant place, wondering quickly what on earth he was doing here.

"Who are you?" he asked nervously.

"Don't you know? I'm the man who called you. Glad you could make it, Mister Seymour . . ."

The man stepped forward, two quick paces, bringing him out into the open slightly so that Jack Seymour could see the smile, the narrowed eyes, the way he seemed poised, like an animal, to spring.

Jack hauled himself to his feet, suddenly terrified. He felt menaced, threatened. He felt in danger, sudden, intense danger.

"Who *are* you?" he shouted, and the man laughed, and started to raise his right arm . . .

A dark wind blew, blinding Jack, as if it were loaded with dust. He heard a strange sound from the other man, a startled, unhappy grunt. Through tear-filled eyes, Jack realized that he was about to be attacked . . .

Then a voice, a woman's voice. "Jack! Where are you? What are you doing?"

"Karen!" he shouted, and inside his head a voice whispered, *Damn, damn, she'll have to be hurt. She's in the way. Shouldn't have brought her.* "Karen, I'm here. In the trees."

The wind had dropped. He looked all around, but there was no sign of the man with the stick. And the more he thought about it, the more he wondered if he had been imagining the fear, and the sense of being threatened. He could hear Karen walking along the track, and he went to meet her.

Six

AS, FOR THE second time in three weeks, Brady made his way north, to Medfield, so a grim memory of the last moments of George Campbell's life began to haunt him as he drove...

Campbell had cold-bloodedly attacked him, using the powerful creation of his own mind, and would have killed Brady without conscience, crushing his body to a pulp in instants; only the man's weakness for Ellen Bancroft, a weakness that had caused his attack on *her* to be a sexual assault and not murder, had allowed Brady's life to be saved. That, and Brady's strange, almost incomprehensible talent for "slipping beyond his own body."

That time before Christmas Brady had psychically "wrestled" with the evil projection of George Campbell's imagination. But later, watching Campbell crushed by the most powerful thought-form that Brady had ever witnessed, he had felt helpless, unable to assist, unable to preserve the life of a man who might have known where his family were...

He had begged Campbell to tell him, kneeling beside the man's crumbling body, watching as the flesh was torn from the bone.

"My family. My children. Answer me, Campbell. For the love of God, there's nothing I can do for you now. I beg you to help me. Where is my family? Are they alive?"

And then, as he had listened to the dying breath of the man, he had heard the word, "Alive..." repeated twice.

Brady had felt tears sting his eyes. Dear God, it had to be true.

"Where are they? Where have they been taken? What is to happen to them?"

Campbell had forced himself upright, and his wretched face came close to Brady's. His foul breath had made Brady wince, but Brady stayed close, willing Campbell to say more.

"Arach . . . awakening . . ." Campbell had gasped. "They've . . . come back . . . power . . . no time . . ."

"I don't understand!"

But Campbell suddenly began to scream, and Brady had stepped back to the door quickly. The man's screeching reached its highest pitch as the thought-form, the mandrathon, had attacked. Campbell had clenched his fists against the sides of his head, which suddenly began to peel, the flesh tearing away from the bone in ragged strips, like a pink banana. The skull still stared, the hands were twisted and snapped by unseen fingers, bones crushed audibly.

Brady had raised his shot-gun and emptied both barrels into the face of the bloody-boned horror that had once been a man . . .

It had been a savage, awesome way to die, Brady's compassion, at the last, overcoming his bitter hatred for the man. But he felt no such hatred for Judith Campbell, who had been unaware of her husband's involvement with the cult.

Brady and Andrew Haddingham had visited Judith Campbell days after the death of her husband, and Brady had surreptitiously searched the house while Haddingham had sat and supported the distraught woman downstairs. He had found nothing, no clue, no hint that Alison and his two children might have been kept in the Medfield house for a while.

He returned to that house now, not really sure why, just aware of his unease at the coincidence of Campbell's country house being so close to Wansham, where something was beginning to occur.

At two in the afternoon he pulled off the road and into the driveway of the ivy-colored, Georgian residence, noticing with puzzlement that a sleek, red Rover had been parked outside the garage. It seemed an untypical car for Mrs. Campbell to use.

The signs of grief were still heavily in evidence on Judith Campbell's gaunt, handsome features. She was a tall woman, elegantly dressed and coiffured, her bearing self-assured, almost aristocratic.

"Mister Brady. This is quite a surprise..."

She held the door for Brady, who smiled and stepped into the cool house. Judith Campbell's eyes were still dark with crying, and her hand-shake had been slightly tremulous. She led the way through to the drawing room, as Brady said, "I would have called you by phone, but I've come by on a whim."

"A whim? A good enough reason," said the woman, indicating one of the armchairs. "A drink perhaps...?"

"No. Thank you."

A wood fire burned in the huge, open grate, the smoke drawn up by the draught that Brady could feel coursing across the room. There was none of the usual, pleasant wood smell. Rather, he could catch a hint of perfume, and yet Mrs. Campbell was wearing none.

"I'm on my way to Wansham," he explained. "I know this is going to sound odd, but I've been directed there after consulting a medium." Mrs. Campbell showed no surprise, her expression one of interested solemnity. She regarded Brady steadily, her hands clasped in her lap, her body perched uncomfortably on the edge of a seat. Brady went on, "I'm looking for my children. I believe I told you that before. It's a long shot, but I think there's a chance they may have been taken through the village of Wansham on their way... wherever. They may even be there still. Since George..." He hesitated, feeling a moment's hatred, a moment's revulsion, as the image of George Campbell was forced into his mind's eye...

What that man had done! Such ferocity, such cruelty! But Judith could not be held responsible. Her feelings had to be protected...

"Since George what?" she prompted, frowning slightly.

"His death, as I think you know, we talked about this before, but his death may have been caused by the same people who took my family, and who tried to kill me..."

"I do know that, yes. At least," she shook her head wearily, "I am aware that the police *believe* there may be a connection."

"Unwittingly, George may have had contact with them. Unwittingly, *I* certainly did. I'm intrigued by how close your house is to Wansham. All I wanted to ask, really, was did George ever go there, ever speak of Wansham? Is there any possibility of a connection between him and the town that might give me a lead?"

"On where to look, you mean?"

Brady nodded. He hoped his words had sounded genuine enough. It was a *very* long shot, and he didn't want his request to sound so odd that the woman, bearing her grief so well, might be given cause to grieve more deeply.

"I really can't think of anything," she said after a moment. "George was involved in many things, mostly in Buckinghamshire. He toured this area, he knew several people. I could give their names to you. I'm sure they wouldn't mind. But this house was our retreat. I've retreated here completely, now. We came here for solitude, not for social activity or work. We were always very insular when we were here. It's something to do with the fens, with the distance between towns. The place is remote; its breeds remote people. I like that remoteness, and so did George."

"So the name of Wansham rings no bells with you at all."

Mrs. Campbell shook her head almost sadly, almost reluctant to be so unable to help.

Behind Brady, a woman's voice said, "He went there twice. About a month ago."

Brady stood and turned. The young woman who was walking into the room from the kitchen was tall, slim and quite exquisite to regard. She wore a pleated skirt and white blouse; her fair hair was cut in the modern style, and her lips were rouged; with her cheeks and eyes touched with colour, she might have stepped off the front cover of *Vogue*. She reached out her hand to greet Brady unsmilingly.

Judith Campbell said, "This is my daughter Melissa. Melissa, Mister Brady worked with George at Hillingvale."

The cool, firm hand was withdrawn from Brady's, and the girl's eyes surveyed him evenly. "Yes, I know. I've heard of you. I'm sorry we didn't meet before; when you came."

"So am I." He was thinking, *how could I have failed to know that Campbell had a daughter? Did Haddingham know?*

"My mother was glad of your visit. It's been a very difficult few weeks."

"I'm sure."

Brady knew that it would have been appropriate to say something about Melissa Campbell's father, some word of sorrow, some expression of sympathy. He could not bring those hypocritical words to the fore, however, and remained awkwardly silent until Melissa asked, "What is so important about Wansham?"

Briefly, Brady explained the tenuous connection between the village, his family, and the disappearance of a business man called John Keeton. Melissa watched him cooly, then glanced at her mother, who sat staring into the wood fire. Reaching out one elegantly manicured hand, Melissa took Brady by the arm and steered him from the room. "We'll look at my father's study. Perhaps we can find a diary entry."

The study was small, claustrophobically crammed with books and teak furniture. Melissa leaned against the desk, watching Brady curiously. Brady found her very beautiful, almost disturbing. She was very together about her father's death; it was as if all the grief were surfacing in Judith Campbell, all the control and organization in the daughter.

"My father visited Wansham twice. I don't know why. I just remember him mentioning it."

"Do you know who he met there?"

The girl shook her shapely head. "No, I don't."

"Or why he went?"

"I couldn't begin to tell you. I live in the North Pennines. I don't visit Medfield very often, and when I do, I huddle. Round the fire. This is the coldest place I know."

There was nothing in any of the scrappy notebooks, incomplete diaries, or box files that cluttered the desk, that could give any indication of George Campbell's business at Wansham, if any. Brady began to get restless, keen to move on to the town, anxious to begin looking. For anything. For a sign.

He excused himself to use the toilet, and when he heard

Melissa Campbell going down the stairs he quickly went through the upper rooms, looking for anything that might suggest people kept there against their will, children in transit. It was a futile gesture, he knew, and he had examined the large rooms carefully that time before, shortly after Campbell's death. All but two of the bedrooms were empty of anything at all. The main room, occupied by Judith Campbell, was furnished simply, a functional and unfussy bedroom for a functional and unfussy woman.

There were only two sheds in the gardens, and they were filled with tools and junk; no room for a rat, let alone a child, or a kidnapped family of three.

Brady was quite certain that if Alison had been brought through this place, she had not managed to leave any sign of it. Campbell had operated from his house in Buckinghamshire, and perhaps had genuinely used the house in the fens as a haven, away from his work and away from the demands, perhaps, of Arachne.

He said goodbye to Judith Campbell, and Melissa walked with him to his car. He was about to take his leave when she reached out and took his arm, turning him to face her. Her eyes bright with an emotion that Brady took to be anger, she said, "What happened to my father? You worked with him. You seem to know what happened better than most people I've spoken to. What *happened* to him, Mister Brady?"

"He was shot; and his house was burned down. What else can I tell you, Melissa? What else is there to tell?"

But she didn't believe him. "I know *how* he died. But what *happened*? Was he involved with something? Who could have done such a vile thing to him? He wasn't the most loved man I know, but he certainly wasn't hated. Not so much that he would be killed so grotesquely."

What do I say? Brady wondered. He stared at the girl, and he could feel the anger in her, the bitterness; he could feel the hate, hate for whatever and whoever had destroyed her family. It was an emotion that radiated from her, and mingled with the hate that Brady himself kept well under control.

He said, "I think the same people who tried to kill me, once, and who took my family, also killed your father."

"Who are they?" she whispered. "Tell me who they are!"

"I'll tell you when I find them. If I knew who they were, I wouldn't be here now. I have very little to go on; clues, yes; hints, yes. Very little substantial. I'm hunting them, Melissa, and when I find them . . ."

The grip on his arm squeezed tighter; she stepped closer, her breath sweet on his face, scented. "When you find them, I want to know why they killed my father. When you find them, I want them to be hurt. I want them really hurt, Mister Brady. As they hurt my mother, as they must have hurt my father before they killed him . . ."

Brady closed his fingers over her warm hand, gently detached her grip from his arm, and turned the gesture into a departing handshake. He said, "I have to find them, first. They're powerful; they're skilled. And they have something very precious to me—my family—and I must beware of jeopardizing those lives. I *will* let you know. I *will* be back . . ."

Impressed by her urgency, by her controlled grief, by her concern for her mother, Brady had decided that he owed the innocents of the family at least that much. It was he who had blasted Campbell into hell, even though Campbell had been dying at the time, being visibly torn apart by one of the most powerful thought-forms imaginable. He could never admit—to anyone—precisely what his role had been in the dispatching of the evil man who had been Melissa's father. But he could permit her the satisfaction of believing, eventually, that Campbell's murderers had been effectively crushed.

Brady continued his drive to Wansham, across the flat, uninviting fen landscape, the minor road along which he had been directed by Melissa Campbell, running straight, occasionally lined by wind-battered trees. There was scarcely any traffic at all on this country lane and he made good time. The scattered farmhouses and tiny villages seemed almost to huddle with cold on the exposed terrain, and Brady was glad when the land rose slightly and a more enclosed countryside appeared.

Five miles from the sea, and from the town, he saw a youth walking along the roadway, rucksack slung across his shoulder. It was a wet day and the man was draped in a short oilskin cape. As he heard Brady's car approaching he turned, peered at the vehicle, then stuck out his thumb.

Brady slowed the Escort to a stop and leaned over the passenger seat to wind down the window. "I'm stopping at Wansham."

The young man peered in through the window. He appeared to be what Brady thought of as a leftover from the sixties, and what Alison had always termed a Californian Cutie: youthfully thin, untrimmed, straggly beard, and with his fair hair parted in the middle and drawn back into a pigtail. His face and hair were saturated with rain, and his small round-framed glasses were splashed with droplets.

Behind the glasses, grey eyes fixed Brady with a searching, intelligent stare. "That's my destination too."

"Get in. We can't be more than five miles."

"Much appreciated." He opened the door and slung his backpack across to the rear seats, then shrugged off his oilskin cape and eased his lanky body into the car. He smelled of sweat and rain; and slightly, Brady realized, of dope.

"First car in an hour. Who wants to visit Wansham?"

"Hazards of hitching," said Brady, and started off again. The hiker began to roll a joint, sniffing loudly several times, and drying his hands on his faded jeans. The inside of the car steamed up, and the ripeness of the youth's unwashed body began to make Brady feel glad that Wansham was only a few minutes away.

Lighting up the thin, economical joint, the boy passed it to Brady. "You smoke?"

"Not any more. Thanks all the same."

"Mind if I do?" He drew on the cigarette before Brady could answer, making that peculiar hissing sound and closing his eyes. Brady glanced at him and couldn't help smiling thinly. The boy was like a drowned rat, and probably frozen; his smelly desert boots and jeans seemed quite dry, but were caked in mud, presumably from nights spent sheltering in the corners of fields. Brady couldn't deny him this brief moment of relaxation and pleasure. He didn't respond to the empty question he had been asked.

"Hitching holiday?" said Brady, curious as to why anyone

should be making their way to so desolate a part of Norfolk so early in the season. "Or are you on some sort of outward bound stamina test?"

"Outward bound?" said the youth, and laughed. "Not me, man. That's for jerks."

Brady grimaced at the Americanization of the boy's Midlands accent. It was an affectation, that use of the word "man," that he had not heard from a white youth for years. The boy suddenly reached across a muddy-fingernailed hand, proffered for shaking, and announced, "My name's Keeton. Alan Keeton. I appreciate the ride."

Tentatively, Brady shook the damp limb. "Dan Brady," he said. "You're welcome." Then the coincidence struck him and he looked sideways at the boy, frowning. "Keeton? That's twice in a day..."

"Twice what in a day?" Keeton drew on the joint again, hissing air into his lungs and holding his breath.

"Twice that I've met that name." Too much, thought Brady. Too much of a coincidence. There *is* something happening. Wansham is a focus, a beckoning point. He felt his excitement rising.

"Where was the first time? Papers?"

"This morning. An item in the *Telegraph* about a businessman who disappeared. He was on holiday in Wansham."

The car passed through an expanse of flood-water, and sheets of muddy spray rose on either side of the speeding chassis.

Alan Keeton said, "My father. John Albert Keeton. I didn't know it had found its way to the papers."

The car was filled with the sour aroma of drugs, and Brady wound down a window, then slowed the car and pulled off the road. He turned off the engine and stared out across the slightly rolling landscape, dark fields made darker beneath the lowering sky. Rain dribbled against the windscreen. Brady shook his head, trying to think clearly about what might have been going on in Wansham. The connection he was eager to make was that John Albert Keeton's disappearance—murder —was part of the same process that had caused the disappearance of Alison, Marianna and Dominick: the work of

Arachne, or Arachne's travelling Collectors. But it was equally important not to start finding similarities, not to start creating the clues he sought...

He didn't know why he had stopped the car, and when Keeton commented, Brady said, "I just need to think for a moment."

"Think on, man. Sure you won't smoke?" The youth's eyes sparkled, and Brady thought there was something cool and calculated about his passenger. There seemed to be little love or concern for the vanished man radiating from this pig-tailed cutie.

"How did you hear about your father?"

At last a touch of feeling entered Keeton's face, and his gestures. He held the smoking joint away from his face, stared through the windscreen, then lowered his gaze to the cigarette. "I was hitching down to join them. A sort of surprise visit. But I called my mother at the hotel. She was hysterical, really uptight by the old man doing his disappearance trick."

"What were they doing in the town?"

Keeton shrugged, glanced at Brady. "I feel distant from them. I'm not that close. Closer to my mother. If she's fucked up, I care. You know what I mean?"

"Yeah, sure," said Brady, quietly mimicking Keeton's lazy drawl. The boy hadn't answered his question. Keeton's eyes narrowed with irritation, but Brady just stared hard at him, and after a second Keeton relaxed, with a wry laugh.

"Okay, so I sound cruel. I've not lived at home for ten years. I've been home, what, three times? I see my mother regularly, my father thinks I'm a freak. Right? So for the first time in years we get together for a holiday, the three of us. Two weeks last summer. Right here, at Wansham. What a fucking place for a family to try and get it together again!"

"What happened?"

Keeton shrugged, drew quickly on the joint, then reached out to stub the smouldering tip into extinction. "The holiday was bad, man. I mean, really bad, you know? Not a word. Real tension. I left after one week, I mean, what else? Nothing but walking and shivering and sitting drinking tea. No speak. No communicate. Too much, man. So I left. The old man was freaked by something, something he found, someone he spoke to. He was different; he changed halfway through that week."

"And he came back to Wansham off-season. Why would he do that, do you think?"

Keeton shrugged. His grey eyes seemed totally alert despite the drug, and he cast nervous, searching little glances at Brady, as if he sensed that Brady knew more than he was letting on, which of course, Brady did. Keeton said, "As far as I know, the old man *had* to come back. Obsessed with the place. My mother didn't want to come, but she agreed. And for her trouble, he goes missing. Walked out on her, I expect; he'll turn up."

I wish for your mother's sake that were true. Brady's thought must have cast a shadow across his face, or perhaps he sighed, or perhaps his failure to respond sympathetically and encouragingly gave Alan Keeton cause to be suspicious. Brady was suddenly aware of the intensity of his passenger's gaze.

"What do you know, Mister Brady? And why are you going to Wansham anyhow? Police? Private D?"

"A little of the latter," Brady said.

"What d'you know about my father?" prompted Keeton.

Brady thought hard and fast. His belief that John Keeton was dead was based on the *impression* held by Angela Huxley that someone had violently entered the spirit world of the Hinterland at about the same time as Keeton was disappearing from the fenland village. By no means a hard and fast confirmation that the elder Keeton had been killed.

He said, "A few months ago my wife and children disappeared."

"From Wansham?"

"No. Not from Wansham."

Keeton looked blank, shaking his head slowly. "So . . . so what? What about my father?"

"I'm hunting the people who took my family," said Brady. "The hunt is bringing me here. It's bringing me here a few days after your father disappeared and I don't like coincidences."

"You think he may have been kidnapped?" Keeton

frowned, trying to get his own thoughts in order, searching Brady's eyes with an intensity that unnerved the older man. "Who? Kidnapped by who?"

I must tell him, Brady thought. I can't converse about kidnapping when I'm convinced that it's murder. I must tell him.

"Maybe Satanists," he said, "or something like. A group of people, an organization. Occultists of some sort. Practitioners of an art that we might call Black, they would call Secret. Evil people. An organization dedicated to an end which I don't yet understand, but which involves kidnapping, ritual . . . even murder at times."

Silence. Alan Keeton was watching him, his lips slightly parted, his eyes wide. Suddenly he smiled, then laughed, briefly, abruptly.

"Are you kidding?"

"I wish I was."

Keeton shook his head, laughed again. "You're crazy. Black magic! Secret arts! What the hell are you trying to pull? This is the twentieth century, man! That stuff ceased to be taken seriously centuries ago."

"I wish that was true too."

The youth watched him carefully, and slowly the look of amused cynicism vanished from his face. "I don't believe you."

"Then start trying," said Brady quietly. Keeton turned away from him, staring through the windscreen. It seemed to Brady that now a degree of understanding was registering in the young man's mind, and that cold, hard shock was beginning to make him care a little more for his estranged father.

"Murder," he said. "Black magic murder. My father . . ." he glanced at Brady, then frowned. "I can't . . . I *can't* believe it. It's too weird. It makes no sense . . ."

"It's a possibility that I urge you to bear in mind, Alan. I agree with everything you say. I share every sentiment of doubt and astonishment and disbelief . . . except that cold, hard experience has tempered my reason."

"Satanists! Devil worship. What the hell was my father up to if that *is* the case?"

"A group *like* Satanists, but I don't think they are. Ritual, yes, and control of elements of the supernatural certainly.

They are called Arachne. They are gathering lives, and they waste the lives of those who aren't needed."

At mention of the word Arachne, Keeton's youthful features had registered a sort of surprise. Brady asked, "Does that word, Arachne, does it mean anything to you?"

Keeton shook his head. "Should it?"

"You looked as if you recognized it."

"Arachne," said Keeton. "Spiders. Weaving a web. Perhaps my father did say something about it, but it means nothing. What about you? What do you know about Arachne?"

Brady shrugged. "Just what I've told you. They are gathering lives, for some purpose that I haven't divined, except that someone, or something, is Awakening. They infiltrated the very highest level of a certain Ministry. I believe they are powerful, very powerful, not just in terms of paranormal talent, but to the degree with which they have already established themselves."

Keeton shook his head, almost wistfully. Brady started up the car and began to drive the last mile or two to Wansham. As the car bumped back onto the roadway, Keeton said, almost in a whisper, "And you're hunting them. One man alone against something so powerful."

"That's right," said Brady quietly, even though he was thinking: *not so alone; I have two or three good friends helping, even if one of them* is *a ghost*. "I shall find them too," he added. "And if my family have not survived..." the thought was too bitter to contemplate, and he snapped his words off, smiling, and adding only, "I *shall* find my family."

"But you're only one man. What makes you think you have any chance at all of surviving once you track down this... Arachne? You have some secret weapon or something? Psychic talent of your own? Psychic talent, man!" He seemed to realize suddenly what he was saying, that he was talking blithely about the paranormal. He smiled thinly as he watched the road. "Listen to me."

Brady just said, "Love and Hate. Love for my family. Hate for the Collectors. What more do I need?"

SEVEN

LATER THAT AFTERNOON Brady took a leisurely, distracted stroll through the silent village. He began at the petrol station that marked the southern edge of the township and walked back along the high street, watching the spartan traffic and the huddled shoppers without any real belief that he would see a sign of anything suspicious.

Wansham's main street was narrow and lined by shops that catered more for a between-wars generation than for modern living: drab clothes shops, grocers whose main stock consisted of biscuits and dry, dull cheese, antique shops staffed by grey-haired women, whose windows were awash with brass and copper trivia. Brady felt an immense weight of desolation as he braved the damp wind, following the high street as it curved out towards the sea, before looping back inland and eastwards to the next dull Norfolk village.

He walked through the churchyard of St. Magnus's, lingering at several of the gravestones, reading names, looking for something, anything, that would prompt an idea. The church was grey, and unusually structured, a cruciform building in early Norman style. It was locked, of course. Even in so remote an area, the destructive hand of youth could impart eternal graffiti to the precious coldstone walls.

He walked on, through the trees and across two fields, one with the beginnings of corn showing through the glistening water-logged earth. He was soon at the seabluff, standing against the bracing wind, and watching the play of cloud and

light across the restless mass of the North Sea. Behind him the
village was a huddle of houses, half obscured by trees. The
road wound out across the landscape, and lights told of farms
and isolated buildings. Everything he saw from this high van-
tage point spoke of desolation, loneliness, a weary isolation
from the main course of English life.

He shivered inside his leather windcheater. The wind made
sounds in the trees and across the earth, sounds like calling
voices, the words an agonizing reminder of the calling of his
children, and of Alison. An image of Alison was powerfully
present in his mind as he walked along the bluff for a while.
He could see her, hair blown by wind, crouched against the
storm, laughing, teasing him, running from him as he chased
after her. Her slim body seemed to dart through his peripheral
vision; he imagined he could feel the texture of her skirt, the
way she would shake her hips as he touched her, as if his
fingers were tickling her flesh.

Alison! God how he missed her!

An hour later, the light was so bad it was becoming dangerous to walk anywhere but on the clearly marked pathways. He
was still following the line of the bluff, but could see that it
had curved around the coast, and was bringing him back to
the road. It was two miles or more to the village from here, a
brisk half hour's walk. He was hungry and cold; he needed a
drink, but drink was one way of reducing one's defence
against psychic attack, and he was never sure when, or how,
he might suddenly come under such an attack.

George Campbell, the man sent to assassinate him was
dead; but he couldn't believe that Arachne would let it rest
there. They would send another thought-form against him,
one day, one week, one month...

There was a farm quite close, a cosier looking block of
buildings than most of the scattered structures he had seen
across the land. Beyond it, on a ridge of ground that vanished
to the south, he could see arc lights, tents and a slow activity
that suggested some sort of excavation. As he stepped onto the
road, staring into that dim distance, a mud-smeared and very
old Cortina was forced to brake quite sharply. Brady stepped
back quickly, calling his apology. A weather-beaten face

peered out at him, a man in his middle age, the life of this bleak farm marked out in every line on his skin, in the furrows and narrows of his brow and cheeks. "Mister Seymour, is it?" he said, then peered harder at Brady. "No, I can see you're not. Thought you were someone else..."

Before Brady could speak, or respond, the car roared away, turning into the gates of the farm, and bouncing and splashing up to the house. Brady had rapidly been thinking of asking for the courtesy of a lift back to the village in exchange for a pint of beer, but he had not had the chance. He shrugged, not particularly bothered and was about to begin walking along the road when a girl's voice called, "Hi!"

He turned to see who had addressed him. She must have been up on the bluff as well; she was picking her way across the fencing by the road, and her tight jeans were mud spattered and sodden. She was wearing a short anorak top, and a bush hat which she removed as she walked up to Brady, smiling. She was short and quite pretty, teenaged, her skin still smooth, her eyes lively, interested, not yet wearied by experience. She was very shapely, very easy in manner, obviously very keen to talk.

"Hi," said Brady.

"A new face," she said. "Not a bad new face either."

"You live in Wansham, do you?"

"God no. Live here? I'm bored out of my skull already, and I've been here precisely three weeks. What's your name?" She was refreshingly direct. She was wearing a perfume that Brady didn't find particularly stimulating, but felt had been freshly applied. He was flattered.

"Dan Brady. Holidaymaker."

"Anita Herbert. Archaeologist's daughter and general dogsbody."

Brady glanced up to the ridge. "Over there?"

Anita shivered as she agreed. "Mud, stones, depression; *and* my father's in a terrible mood."

"Why stay?"

"I promised. I'm also earning money to go to America. I'll do anything for a plane ticket to the States, even break my nails."

"Boyfriend over there?"

She smiled, her eyes twinkling mischievously. "More than one."

Brady glanced again at the excavations. "What are they digging? What are *you* digging, I should say."

"It's an old settlement, eighth century. Saxons and Angles, and Norse intrusions later on. It's mostly post holes, rubbish pits, and some bone. Walk with you to the town?"

"How about taking me up to the ridge? I'd like to see the site."

"You're joking! Tell me you're joking. There's nothing to see."

"I'm not joking. I'm interested," said Brady, trying to be light-hearted. "Take me up to the site and I'll buy you a drink later on."

"Where're you staying?"

"Where else? The Royal Oak."

"It's busy for off-season. A man got lost here a day or so back. The bluff was crawling with police. New people have come to stay at the farm here too. Can't imagine what the attraction of this grotty place is. It never stops raining."

Brady had started walking towards the edge of the field which led to the ridge. Anita was walking along beside him; she suddenly stopped. "You sure you want to see this?"

"Quite sure."

The mud was sticky, clinging. They picked their way carefully around the field, and made the easy ascent to the higher ground. Brady could not understand why a settlement would have been set up in so exposed a place, unless there had been a defensive advantage. But the wind fairly ripped at his clothes and hair as they got to the roped-off edge of the dig.

Anita had been right. There was little to see. The turf had been peeled back over several strips and squares and the dirt removed to a depth of several feet, exposing the rainwashed grey rock. The rock appeared pitted with holes, although Brady's overwhelming impression of the dig was of polythene sheets, flapping white labels, and the sound of canvas being stretched against the storm.

One younger man was crouched above a patch of ground using a trowel to move mud. He was unaware of Brady and

Anita, who stood huddled behind him, watching his rainproofed form dedicatedly applied to the task of clearing out post-holes.

"Satisfied?" said Anita, the sound of her voice making the working man look round in surprise, then acknowledge her. He stood. He had a thin, pinched face with deep-set, grey eyes. He didn't smile as he was introduced as Simon Moss, and shook Brady's hand. He turned back to his work and Anita said, "See? Boring, isn't it?" Brady wasn't sure if she meant Simon Moss or the work he was doing.

From one of the two tents an older, more distinguished looked man appeared. He glanced suspiciously at Brady, then smiled and came across to them. He was holding a polythene bag with fragments of what looked like metal in them. "Seen your father?" he asked, as he came up to them.

"Not for hours," said the girl. "A new face," she went on by way of introducing Brady. "Dan Brady. He asked for a look at our work. This is Doctor Ewen Holbrook."

Brady and Holbrook shook hands briefly. Holbrook raised the bag he carried. "Axe heads. Evidence of quite a fight here. Impossible to gauge when exactly, of course, but probably eighth century." Brady thought how typical of the stereotype of an English archaeologist Holbrook looked, with his half-lenses, longish white hair, slightly absent-minded manner; a man whose mind was on other things than what he was saying.

"A fight between who? Saxons and Vikings?"

"Something like that," said Holbrook, pleasantly patronizing. "This area was widely settled by the Germanic Angles. East Anglia . . . it's where the name comes from. The Norse were very active down this coast, so yes, it's quite likely that Uffricshame fell to the swords of the Danes."

The word Uffricshame sent a sudden shiver down Brady's spine; he recognized that name from the seance session with Angela Huxley. "What does Uffricshame mean?"

"The homestead of Uffric's people," said Holbrook matter-of-factly. "We can't be exactly sure that this is Uffric's own settlement, but we have certain clues, certain evidence."

"Uffric being . . . who exactly?"

"A Warlord, an Anglian King," said Holbrook. "He was an honourable man who was dishonoured in some way.

Betrayed by the woman he loved, goes the eleventh century legend about him. We have fragments of records from a monastery, and believe it or not a reference or two in a newly discovered saga. It's the positioning on the ridge that makes us more confident. A fortified settlement, and there is evidence that it was an important man who lived here. Uffric. It has to be." Holbrook glanced quickly at Brady, perhaps to see if Brady was actually interested in the mini-lecture, or just politely listening. Then he looked at Anita. "Where's your father, did you say?"

"I didn't. I don't know."

"Come and give me a hand, would you? Excuse us, Mister . . . ?"

"Brady."

"Mister Brady, it's more fun here when the weather's better. Do come again. Goodbye."

Looking glum, in fact looking downright irritated, Anita Herbert followed Doctor Holbrook into the second tent, leaving Brady to make his own way back to the road, and the village. Her wistful, "See you later?" was acknowledged, on Brady's part, by a smile and a shrug. It would be useful to talk to her, certainly. She seemed to have been prowling around the area, wandering boredly about the village and the bluffs. He was at once wary of her, as indeed he was wary of everyone, but able to recognize her potential usefulness.

There were two uniformed policemen in the lounge of the Royal Oak when Brady finally got back there. He was perished, miserable, and ready for a brandy, despite the ill-advisedness of consuming alcohol. But his own physical discomfort could not mask the atmosphere of tension and unease that pervaded the warm hotel bar.

Voices were low, save that of a woman. Brady saw Alan Keeton sitting in a corner armchair. The loud spoken woman sitting with him was obviously his mother. She was still distressed, but Keeton looked just bored.

The police were in earnest conversation with the manager of the hotel. Brady stepped up to the bar and asked for a drink. The young police officers watched him, then passed him a photograph which showed a man in his middle years, and two teenage girls. "Would this face mean anything to you?"

Brady studied the picture. "What, the man?"

The barman brought him his brandy. Brady shook his head. "I only arrived here this afternoon. Haven't seen him."

"Which way did you come? Main road?"

"No, the B-something-or-other, from Medfield."

"See anybody? Anything stick in mind?"

"Nothing at all. I gave a lift to Alan Keeton," Brady nodded towards the youngster in the corner. The police seemed uninterested in that.

The barman said, "Well all I can say, is I've had about enough. If *you're* thinking of upping and leaving in the middle of the night, I'll thank you to let me know."

"What's happened?" *The second arrival,* he was thinking. *The town has had another disappearance.*

"Bloke came here yesterday, to stay. A week he said. Went out last evening, about this time, not much later. And that's it. Not a sign of him. Just like the other, Keeton there. Two in two days, I ask you! So if you're thinking of following that, Mister Brady, just leave me a note. Never mind your belongings, just a courtesy."

He walked away from the police to serve a regular. The uniformed men stared at Brady, as if searching among their suspicions for a question or two to ask him. Brady initiated a conversation with them, intrigued by what else they might have known. But they knew nothing. They'd been called here by the owner of the hotel, shown the man's room, his belongings, including the photograph, and could do no more than ask questions and search.

Two men vanished in as many days, and it was time to think about bringing in the CID.

"Could they have drowned?" said Brady.

"Most likely," said the more talkative of the two. "People come out this way in winter, they've got to appreciate that it's dangerous to go for country walks. You may be right, Mister Brady. Along the sea bluff, the going is treacherous. Both these men went walking that way, but I don't suppose we'll be dragging the bogs for them. Too many and too deep."

"Odd, though, isn't it?" said Brady, and the policemen looked unanimously puzzled. "Odd? What's odd?"

"All this sudden activity in Wansham. Visitors off-season. Excavation up on the ridge. Strangers in town . . ."

"Strangers? What strangers?"

There had been no strangers, and Brady winced inwardly. He had been fantasizing about prompting a response from the police: ah, yes, *those* strangers, with the woman and the two children.

It had been a feeble effort, although Brady was intrigued by one of the men saying, "It is odd, though. That bloke Keeton, and this man Shackleford. Both of them were here last summer, and both around the same time. Same wouldn't go for you, would it Mister Brady?"

"No, sorry. Any idea why they came back?"

"Keeton was obsessed with the town. His wife's words. He felt that call to return. To this place," the two men laughed and exchanged a glance. After a moment they climbed off their bar stools, pocketed their notebooks, and left the bar. The owner of the hotel—Seb Quinn—walked back to Brady, rolled his eyes and shook his head. "First bit of fuss in Wansham as long as I can remember. Trust the police to be stumped."

"As a matter of interest," Brady said, "in recent weeks, has there been anyone unusual, or anything unusual in the village?"

Frowning, Quinn shook his head, fixing Brady with a stare that smacked strongly of suspicion. "Short of the archaeologists, no. Not that I've noticed. You from the police too, are you?"

"No, I'm not. I'm a private investigator. I'm working for the Keetons, though Mrs. Keeton doesn't know it . . ." Why not? It seemed reasonable.

The publican was impressed. "Like Jim Rockford, eh? Rockford Files."

"Something like that."

"The Brady files," he shook his head. "Not as good." He grinned.

"Unusual people, you asked. The men up on the ridge are unusual. They don't drink. That's *highly* unusual. The girl does, though. Little hussy."

"Anita Herbert?"

"That's the one. You met her, have you? You watch your step, Mister Brady. That one's got a lust for life and the emphasis is on the word..."

He didn't finish the observation, but Brady got the point.

Seb Quinn tapped his forefinger on the counter, looking thoughtful. "Now when it comes to unusual people, there were two women. Called through Wansham getting on for three weeks ago now. They had to do with the archaeologists, I think. Can't be sure, mind you. But they were an odd pair. Not bad looking. Elegant. But *above* it all, if you get my meaning."

Brady nodded in agreement, encouraging him to get to the point. "Funny thing was, they had this odd smell about them. Like wood smoke. Cloying. Like they'd been standing by a bonfire, and the smoke was in their clothes. One of them never spoke. Fingers covered with rings; earrings, necklaces, but not jewels, not what you'd call precious stones."

"More modern, you mean."

But Quinn hadn't meant that at all. "More primitive. Like African jewellery. Stones and dull metal. Very odd."

Talismans, Brady was thinking.

"Did you get their names?"

The barman shook his head. "Didn't ask. They were about the village for a day, and that was it. I saw them over by the sea-bluff, walking. Holidaymakers I expect. Summer haters."

"You just said they were with the excavation team up on the ridge."

"Maybe they were. They had a drink in here with the two doctors. Talked about ghosts, restless spirits. Up on the ridge," he explained as Brady raised his eyebrows questioningly, "we call it the Roozie. Haunted place. Even the girls' seen ghosts up there, and out across the styke."

Exasperated with the local names, Brady smiled and shook his head. "Styke? What's that, the sea-bluff?"

"No, no. The styke's the bogland, stretches ten miles or so to Little Minster."

"Good name. Styke I mean."

"Old name. Means place of drowning, or so the story goes. The people who lived up in the Roozie used the bogs to sacrifice to whatever it was they worshipped, gods, demons, the earth mother." He chuckled. "Earth mother. Round here, we'd say 'mud' mother."

"Have *you* seen ghosts, out on the styke?"

"Maybe. I'm not sure that I'd recognize one if I saw it, though. Most times of the year, the styke is covered with dew-mist. Cows, farmers, even trees can look ghostly. Local superstition will make play with anything it can. There are people in this village, though, and not just the older folk, who won't walk across the styke, or even visit Kett's Farm. That's close-by to where they're digging. Won't go there." The man was enjoying his talk, his voice becoming more and more mysterious as he treated Brady, the visitor, to a verbal tour of Wansham folk-lore. "Those same folk say the styke's more active this last few weeks than for years . . ."

"Ghosts abroad, you mean."

"Aye. I do mean. They blame the archaeologists, disturbing the dead. Most of the old people are down in the crypt of St. Magnus's, dug up years back, but respected, see? Respected. But those two doctors, they're digging without respect. Those who believe in supernatural forces in the area—and I'm not one of them—but those who do, they say there's a disturbance in the area. It's the diggers. That's why they're not liked here. The girl . . ." he looked away in disgust, straightened up from the bar and reached for a bottle of Haig whisky, "she causes disturbances of a different nature."

Brady allowed himself one small, diluted whisky.

It was good storytelling. It was the stuff of tourism, folklore and legend. But to Brady, talk of ghosts, disturbances, women wearing talismans, all of this could not be easily dismissed. Any single fragment of the hotelier's traditional gossiping might have linked with his hunt; with his search.

Eight

KAREN SEYMOUR AWOKE abruptly in the middle of the night, conscious that someone was prowling about the bedroom. Adrenalin coursed through her body, bringing her instantly alert, as she saw the dark shape of the man standing by the window. The glowing dial of the alarm clock showed her that it was just after one in the morning.

She moved her leg gently back, to nudge Jack awake. Her probing foot found only cold sheets and emptiness, and she turned to confirm that her husband was not in bed with her.

All panic drained from her as she realized that the man who had been prowling around the room, walking stealthily, like an intruder, was Jack himself. "What the hell are you doing? It's freezing."

He said nothing. Karen reached out and flicked on the small bed-side lamp. The room was damp and chilly, and Jack Seymour stood naked and goose-pimpled, staring out across the midnight land.

"Can't sleep. Can't sleep," he said, and shivered. His arms were wrapped about his shoulders. His body was not firm, and his buttocks shook as his flesh reacted to the cold. "Put something on you," Karen said, but he shook his head. "Not cold."

"You're freezing!"

He turned on her, his face distorted into an animal-like

snarl, his eyes wide, but hideously cruel. "I said I'm not cold," he shouted and his teeth chattered, making the words tremulous.

Karen swung her legs out of the bed, pulled her thin nightdress down to cover her bare skin, and walked over to him. "Come back to bed, Jack . . ."

Roughly he pushed her away, turned back to the window. Karen felt sadness and despair well up inside her, and she knew that she would start to get hysterical unless she could start to understand her husband. Her hands shook. She knew she must have looked a mess, but she so desperately wanted to reassure him, and to be reassured by him. She reached out to touch him, and the hand she placed on his cold arm was not repulsed. More confidently, she came close to him and reached round his broad chest. "Come to bed, Jack. I want you. I'm wide awake, and seeing you standing there . . ."

It was something she knew about him, that he could respond at the most inopportune of times to brazenness, to an overt declaration of desire on her part. She slid her hand down across his stomach, and stroked his cool flesh. There was an immediate response as she squeezed and gently closed her fingers around him.

"Come to bed." She felt unaroused herself, but knew that she could cope with that. It had suddenly become desperately important to her to have sex with her husband, an affirmation that all was well between them, deep down, under the surface of this madness. They had not had sex for over a month, something that occurred regularly in their relationship, a fluctuating activity that they both accepted.

Now it was time to flip the pendulum back. She squeezed his penis harder, gently biting into his shoulder.

"No!" He flung her off with such violence that she stumbled across the bed and went sprawling.

"Jack!"

He shivered violently, paced up and down the bedroom, not looking at her, not really looking at anything. His gaze seemed focussed on some inner vision, on something outside the walls of the farmhouse. His erection remained, and he looked both odd and terribly threatening as he walked around her, increasingly restless, driven by a fire whose nature Karen could not even guess.

"They're here," he said. "They must be."

"Who's here?"

He said nothing, ignoring her plaintive attempt to communicate with him. Back to the window he went, darkly silhouetted against the partial moonlight. "Why don't they speak? Why don't they come?"

"Who are you waiting for, Jack?" She was thinking of the afternoon, when she had followed him out to the sea-bluff and found him stuck in mud, panic-stricken, white-faced, almost hysterical. She had seen the archaeologist, the old man with the stick, walking up that same way, but he had been nowhere to be seen, and she had had to drag Jack back to his senses, and to safety, on her own. He had been confused, almost angry, even then shrugging off her attentions. He had walked briskly back to the farmhouse, and throughout supper had been sullen, silent, to the irritation of James Hadlee.

Mrs. Hadlee had been sympathetic, recognizing that Karen was being placed under strain by something in her husband's behaviour. Karen felt glad that the old woman was around. She didn't need advice, or assistance, she merely needed the strong presence of the woman, the sympathetic ear. They had talked for an hour, and Karen had done most of the talking, while Jack had gone to bed, sleeping restlessly, his body coated in a sheen of cold sweat.

"Who are you waiting for, Jack?" she asked again, still sitting on the edge of the uncomfortable bed.

It's a feeling, a terrible, irresistible feeling that someone wants to speak to me.

His remembered words were sinister, terrifying. It was as if he had been called back to Wansham to conclude unfinished business. But what business, and with whom?

Who was tugging at the strings of Jack Seymour, making him jerk and twist with restless unease, not knowing what to do, where to go, making him unable to speak to his wife in anything but the most indifferent monosyllable?

"Jack, I'm going to send for an ambulance. You're ill. You're not right. You have some sort of fever."

She didn't mean it, of course. She was trying to provoke response from him.

And response she got.

He turned from the window, snarling through clenched teeth, and rushed at her, knocking her to the floor with a savage slap from his right hand. "Leave me alone! I'll kill you! Shouldn't have come . . . along, don't interfere. Must get back. Must find . . . back . . ."

Each word was said with violence, squeezed out, making an incoherent whole. Karen watched him, and she felt raw terror, deep fear that he would strike again. Her face burned with pain. She was aware only of Jack's narrowed, gleaming animal eyes, and his hands clenched into bone-hard fists, the weapons of a killer.

A moment later he had run from the room. Karen struggled to her feet, listening to his heavy footfall on the stairs. She ran after him, hearing the back door flung open almost frantically.

The night was bitterly cold; a brisk wind blew through her nightdress and she shivered uncontrollably as she walked out into the muddy yard, feeling the dampness penetrate the slippers she had put on her feet. "Jack!" she called, and wondered whether the noise would wake the Hadlees, whom she knew to be heavy sleepers. Should she wake them herself? She glanced up to their room, but the window was dark. The wind whistled through the eaves of the barns and out-buildings. The moon, behind clouds, streaked the dark sky with eerie illumination. She imagined she could hear the crash of the sea against the flats, beyond the sea-bluff.

"Jack, come in. You'll catch your death . . ."

Her mother's remembered words. Everything could cause her to "catch her death." She realized that she was terrified of Jack dying, and that she had a sixth sense nagging at her, a feeling that his life *was* threatened. The thought was almost too much to bear. She thought of Chris, back in Edmonton, upset that his parents had left him for a week, waiting so eagerly for them to come home again.

Ignoring the wet and the cold, Karen walked across the yard to the open door of a barn. There was no sign of Jack anywhere out across the fields, or on the track that led to the road. He must have gone into the barn, madness taking him to warmth.

Two chickens moved sluggishly from the dark confines of the building as she stepped inside. "Jack? Where are you? For God's sake, come back to the house. I mean it, Jack! Jack!"

She stepped forward, feeling straw below her slippers. The place smelled of damp wood and animals.

A movement behind her made her turn with shock, and what she saw there, rushing at her, made her scream with all her might . . .

The sound was stifled by a rough hand, pressed across her mouth. She was flung back onto the straw, her spine twisting painfully. The animal breathing of the man who lay above her, tearing at her night-clothes, was loud in her ears.

"Jack . . . No! Get off me!"

He was like a beast, and his body seemed to glow with a pale, ghastly phosphorescence, his face distorted into something skull-like and grinning. His body flexed, the muscles of his arms appearing huge, powerful, his shoulders broader, stronger. It was not the appearance of the man she had married, and yet it was Jack, it was Jack . . .

His hands ripped off her nightdress, and rough fingers squeezed and dug at her breasts. She struggled to sit, but the hand came back across her throat and mouth, forced her body back to the ground. Cruel fingers thrust between her legs, then stretched open her thighs, the nails raking at her flesh. Teeth sank into her neck, then her right breast, and she knew blood had been drawn from the tender nipple.

He was erect, vibrating with sexual energy, and he forced his way into her with three animal, passionless thrusts, and pounded upon her with a violence and a frenzy that she had never known from this most gentle of lovers. He groaned and cried triumphantly as his seed spurted into her body.

As quickly as he had come he jerked out of her, reached a hand to squeeze the flesh of her bleeding breast, then laughed.

He moved away from her, vanishing from the barn, out into the night. Karen cried bitterly, one hand across her mouth to stifle the sound, the other reaching for the torn nightdress to pull across her raped and frozen body.

• • •

Strong. Strong. The body has power, unrealized power. I need the strength. It can be harnessed. Run! Run! Feel the power!

Jack Seymour paced across the fields, his feet cut on shards of stone, the skin pricked by sharp stubble. The pain was welcome. He laughed at the pain, laughed at the cold. The body was strong, and could be stronger.

As he pushed his muscles to the limit, feeling his limbs ache, his breathing become more controlled, he thought of the bleeding body of Karen, lying in the barn, and tears of anger welled up within him . . .

Repressed, smashed, pushed down again!

Strong, strong!

He crouched in the shelter of a tree, watching the dark night. His breathing was laboured, his lungs tearing apart inside his ribs, but it was an agony that would pass, and he grinned at the thought of pain. He touched a hand to his groin, and raised the fingers to his nostrils, loving the scent of the woman he had taken.

He watched the ridge. He was confused by the darkness. There should be palisade walls, flickering torches. *This was the way they had come, walking from the sea, cold and hungry, wary of the people who had come to greet them, but hopeful that the agreements would be kept. It was a time for feasting, the bond forged between the two peoples* . . .

He was being watched. He was sure he was being watched. From a distance, yes. Through darkness, yes. But watched.

He rose to his feet, and the wind struck him bitterly, and the fleeting images of a torch-lit walk across the bogs faded.

Jack Seymour blinked in astonishment. He looked down at his shivering, naked body, feeling suddenly terribly vulnerable. Then a great surge of shock and disgust hit him, the image of Karen below him, his fingers raking her flesh, the brutal act he had committed upon her . . .

"Karen . . ." he whispered to the night, then more loudly, "Karen!"

What had he done? His mind was clear. The confusion of the preceding minutes had passed away. What in God's name had he *done*? How on earth could he come to be standing in the middle of nowhere, in the middle of the night, totally naked, Karen's blood on his skin?

Wincing with the pain in his feet as he picked his way back across the fields to the farmhouse, Seymour began to weep. His sorrow was evoked by guilt, by fear at the powerlessness he felt when his body reacted so violently, by the pain he had caused Karen, by the knowledge that he was rapidly destroying Karen, and Chris, his whole family. He wept, too, through fear for his life, for he was obsessed with a powerful idea of his own death, now; death was inevitable. And the cause of his death resided within himself, and he could not control it.

—NINE

IT WAS GONE eight in the morning before Brady opened his eyes. He came abruptly awake, and sat up in the deep, uncomfortable bed.

He could have sworn that the door had just been closed, as if someone had been entering and disturbed him, and had swiftly retired.

His head felt heavy. He knew why. For days he had been sleeping fitfully, restlessly, and for a very few hours. Last week, he had driven north, to Yorkshire, on nothing but a whim, and on returning had made this second long trip to Norfolk. He had been thinking, hard and concerned, trying to control grief, and hate, trying to balance his thoughts.

For weeks he had been denying his body its proper repose. It was catching up on him. He was weakening.

Stepping from the bed, he pulled back the curtains, then checked the various defences he had erected around the room, protecting him against the visitation upon his person of a possible psychic attack. Brady had asked specifically that his room should not be made up. He didn't want his tentative defences to be disturbed. There were bowls of vinegar and salt, smears of mandragora and wolfsbane, garlic, of course, and the thick smear of animal fat with which he had marked a circle around the periphery of the room.

Everything was intact. His body, if tired, felt calm. He was experiencing none of the symptoms of being psychically targeted: headaches, anxiety, dizziness, loss of appetite.

If Arachne *was* in Wansham, it was either unaware of his presence here, or watching, waiting, biding its time.

He washed quickly, then dressed and went down to a quite excellent English traditional breakfast, cooked by the landlord himself, who sat and chatted with Brady while he ate.

Mrs. Keeton had been up and out some half hour before, with her appalling exhibition of a son (Quinn's expression) with her.

The day was brighter and drier, still a miserable excuse for Spring, but more cheering for the visitors. Brady retrod his route of the evening before, through the village, through the churchyard, and up to the bluff. It was there that he saw the Keetons. They were standing, looking away from the sea, and when Brady approached, he could hear that Mrs. Keeton was crying.

She wiped her eyes as Brady hailed them. Alan Keeton stared at him unsmiling, his eyes cold and controlled behind his glasses. His long hair was blowing free in the wind. He kept his hands in the pockets of his jeans. "Good morning," said Brady.

"We're retracing my father's steps," said the youth.

Brady smiled at Kath Keeton, who regarded him through tear-blurred eyes and gave him a wan little smile back. "I'm very sorry about what's happened," said Brady.

"But I don't *know* what's happened," the woman said, and her lower lip quivered for a moment. "If I knew . . . If I knew he was dead, or alive, or wandering. But not to know . . ." Her voice was almost a whine.

Alan Keeton touched her arm sympathetically, reassuring her. "We'll find him. Don't worry so much. The way you two fight, he's bound to just have gone off and sulked."

Brady asked, "Where did you last see him?"

Kath pointed further along the sea-bluff. "We walked here. It was cold and rainy, and we'd parked the car at the bottom of the track. I turned and came back to the car and the last I saw, John was standing over by those trees."

She was indicating a tight-knit copse, of the sort that could conceal a mire.

"The police had a good look over there," said Alan. "If he went down, that's it. No way we'll ever find him."

"Alan!" said his mother bitterly. "He can't have done. He wouldn't be so careless!"

"See you later," said Brady. "Don't get cold."

Alan glanced at him and shrugged. He led his mother back towards the village, walking slowly, his arm on her shoulders.

Brady walked over to the boggy clump of trees, and felt the way the ground became soft, then sucking. There was a gurgling sound all around, water bubbling and sinking through the turf. It was eerie and unpleasant, and it made him wary of even the most solid-looking pieces of ground.

He walked among the trees, climbed across the wire fence, and stepped cautiously around the almost invisible mire. Something about the place excited him, disturbed him. It was not a presence, not a feeling of the place watching him, so much as a feeling that an event of importance had occurred here. The sheltered wood fairly vibrated with life, with energy, an echo of life, perhaps an echo of death.

It had been here. Brady was sure of it. Every prickling hair of his neck, every crawling inch of his skin, told him so.

He crouched and looked around. A branch, trailing out across the green, muddy surface of the bog itself, was chipped. Mud had covered the bright scar on the wood, which could be seen clearly when he used another piece of dead wood to scratch the dirt away. A knife had cut that branch. Bog mud had splattered the trunks of the trees some feet from the mire. He recognized it, dried, yes, but of a different colour and texture to the firmer ground around the trees.

There had been a struggle. Someone had splashed in the mud and water of the sucking pit.

Brady turned back, still crouching, to scan the surface of the mire, looking for anything, a fragment of clothing, footprints in the soft bank. The police would have made only a cursory inspection of the place, assuming that if he had gone down, he was lost; and if he hadn't, he would turn up elsewhere. Murder would not have occurred to them.

As his gaze roamed the bog, he saw it. He stood upright with a gasp of disgust, and shock, then leaned forward a little to be sure that he was not mistaken.

It looked just like a lump of grey faecal matter, floating on the mud. But when he looked close, he could see the curled fingers of a human hand, severed at the wrist.

Brady never doubted for an instant that the severed hand belonged to either Keeton or Shackleford; one or both of them were down in the mud, and Brady was equally confident that Arachne—or its representatives working in this area—had put them there.

But was that group still here, or had they moved on? The strange women had passed through the town weeks ago, yet the deaths were recent.

As he strolled along the road, Brady watched the Roozie. Four strangers, four people who had been here longer than any other visitor. Four people disturbing the balance of forces in the area, upsetting the ghosts of Wansham.

It seemed too obvious, on the one hand, to assume that so innocent and drab an excavation might conceal the evil practice of a group of occultists. And yet . . .

He watched the movement up on the ridge. The two women had talked with the man, or men, in charge of the dig. But there was practically nothing suspicious about the girl, Anita Herbert, nothing beyond the obvious suspicion that she might not have been in full control of her budding sexuality.

The group on the ridge interested him, intrigued him. They spoke to his deeper awareness; they were too obvious, yes. But Arachne *was* obvious; its members were arrogant. They had arrogantly invaded his home in December; months before, they had attacked Ellen Bancroft, and she had lived in a block of flats, and her screams had alerted everyone around. Whoever was hiding behind the masks of the Collectors, they were confident enough in their power, or their anonymity, that they didn't make great efforts to conceal themselves.

Doctors Herbert and Holbrook, Anita Herbert and the arrogant-looking young man, Simon Moss. Brady wanted to know more about them, but at the moment he could hardly go up to them and challenge them directly. He had no proof. They could play it dumb, and he would have nothing with which to break them down . . .

But one of them, perhaps more than one, might have been in his house on that December night. Those quiet, intellectual eyes might have regarded him through the sockets of the foul

animal masks, and coldly instructed *Kill him*. One among
them may have carried the limp body of his daughter out into
the garden, and away into the darkness.

And if that were the case, then the bog at the bottom of the
sea-bluff would soon claim new life. Brady promised himself that as he walked thoughtfully back to the Royal Oak to
find something to eat, to ponder the best way of seeking for
Arachne among the people digging at Uffricshame.

The rest of the day passed by without incident, but with increasing frustration on Brady's part. He had longed to be able
to *smell* the evil presence in the village, to be able to sense it;
but his only talent, if talent it was, was for detaching his spirit
from his body—undergoing an out-of-the-body experience at
times of great stress; Ellen Bancroft had been psychic to a
degree whereby she might have been *acutely* aware of the ex-
istence of Arachne within the tiny focus of Wansham, but he
was not.

He explored the church, finding it dull, lifeless, a typical
spiritually deserted building, probably used only for harvest
festivals. He didn't bother with the crypt, whose key he had
not thought to acquire in any case.

At three o'clock he followed Doctor Ewen Holbrook, by
car, out into the wilds of the fens, a distance of two miles. He
tried to be discreet but it wouldn't have taken a Jim Rockford
to realize that he was being followed when there was practically no traffic at all on the winding country road. Holbrook
was merely fetching two boxes of equipment from a small,
miserable looking house, that stood on its own in an over-
grown untended garden.

This, Brady established after Holbrook had left, was where
the four of them were staying, "commuting" the distance to
the Roozie every day. It was a two-bedroomed cottage, practically bare of furniture. Brady gained entry through the
kitchen window and walked through every room, but the place
was merely a sleeping post, with cotbeds, basic kitchen sup-
plies, and several tables pulled together, now covered with an
elaborate plan-map of Uffric's settlement.

Nothing occult. No sign of talismans, black candles, wax
images, animal masks or robes.

Brady sprawled out in one of the high-backed wooden

chairs, closed his eyes and tried to summon images of Alison and his two children. The images came, but were not accompanied by any residual, echoing psychic disturbance in the tiny cottage. *Damn*. He realized that his fists were clenched, the futility of this aimless searching beginning to nag at him badly.

Where have they taken them? Where have they taken them?

Before anger and frustration could cause him to damage property, and thus perhaps draw attention to himself, he left the cottage, and drove back to Wansham. He sat in his room, staring out of the window, across the red-tiled roofs to the just-visible distant bluff. He knew that somehow, and very soon, he was going to have to force the issue. He was going to have to draw attention to himself, and perhaps provoke a response—almost certainly an attack—from Arachne, if its followers were indeed in the area.

If Dan Brady possessed no intrinsic psychic power, he was nonetheless equipped with a reasonable degree of premonition. He had *known* that the girl would come, and at about six o'clock, when the light was fading, and the wind increasing outside, he sensed powerfully that she was on her way to him.

Sure enough, at six-thirty someone rapped gently on the door of his room, and when he called, "Come in," Anita Herbert stepped quickly, almost surreptitiously into the room.

"Hi."

"I've been expecting you."

She was wearing a short black skirt with net stockings that couldn't hide the fact that her legs were still slightly chubby in a post-pubescent way. Through her loose white blouse, Brady could see that her breasts were large and unsupported. She had pinned her dark hair back across one ear, and her eyes sparkled with mischief. "Do you have a corkscrew?" she asked, and raised the bottle of Beaujolais she had brought. Brady didn't, and went down to the bar to fetch one; he also brought up glasses. When he got back to his room, Anita was seated on the side of the bed, legs crossed in a clearly provocative way.

Brady smiled at that. "Like me, do you?" he said coolly, as he poured wine into the glasses. Anita watched him, a smile touching her lips.

"Yes, I do."

"How old are you?" He passed her a glass, and raised his own. The wine was bitter.

"Twenty-four," she said quickly, and Brady laughed, shaking his head.

"I doubt it."

"Twenty," she corrected, looking at him over the rim of her glass as she sipped the wine. "In two months time."

"I'm thirty-five," said Brady. "Don't you think . . . ?"

"I don't think anything," she said quickly. "I just react, respond. I see someone I like, I like them. I don't start defining the edges: age, weight, marital status."

Brady sat down on the wide window ledge, watching the girl, who leaned back on the bed, so that she was half way across it. Brady said, "Well, you're refreshingly frank, I'll give you that."

"This town's a drag," she said. "Definitely a drag, and there's nothing until you get to Cromer that you could call fun. And even Cromer's boring. It's just that it's on a bigger scale." She sipped wine, staring at Brady. "You're the most interesting new face to come to Wansham."

"What about the hippie?"

She made a retching noise, her nose literally wrinkling. "What a freak. More wine, please." She held out her glass, and Brady obliged.

"You're all living out on the Minster road. Your team, I mean. Is that right?"

She grimaced, almost shivering. "What a dump. Why they couldn't have arranged to stay at Kett's Farm I don't know. Farmer Hadlee didn't like the look of them, if you ask me. Who *would* like the look of my father? Miserable old bugger." She smiled sweetly. "You're not really on holiday, are you?"

Brady shook his head. He had no idea at all how to play the next few minutes. He wanted information from the girl . . . and he wanted the girl. Despite her overt posturing, he felt desire for her. It was perhaps no more than a response to the weeks of abstinence, following years of a regular and satisfying relationship with Alison. But if she knew something of the mysterious group called Arachne—or if she was a part of that group—he couldn't let her go without getting an idea of that fact.

"No, I'm not on holiday," he said quietly.

"What then?" Her gaze at him was interested, suggestive, entirely innocent, and it disturbed Brady.

"I'm looking for something."

"What? What could one possibly come to Wansham to look for?"

"*You're* part of it."

She smiled and wiggled her hips as she lay on the bed. "That's nice. More of that, please."

She had responded innocently, selfishly.

"I'm looking for Arachne."

"Arachne who? Is she pretty?" It was a tease, and Anita smiled almost apologetically. "Sorry. What's Arachne? Spiders. You're a zoologist, and you're looking for rare spiders. I see. Come over here and let me weave my web around you. *That's* a rare treat."

"Arachne is an occult group. I don't know how else to describe them."

Anita Herbert looked baffled. "You mean like witches? You've come looking for witches?" She wriggled with pleasure, then sat up. "That *is* fun. Have you been up to St. Magnus's? There's a *terrible* atmosphere in the place. Definite associations with witchcraft. Wansham is a really haunted town. Did you know that? Every house has a ghost. The Roozie is haunted too. I've seen it. So you're a ghost hunter. Can I come with you when you go hunting? My father will create hell, but I can't help that . . ." her rapid patter died away as she noticed that Brady wasn't responding, or reacting, just staring at her.

Brady said quietly, "Arachne is people. Many people. Powerful people, with psychic talents beyond belief. I had a wife. I had two lovely children. Those people took them. They raped my wife, and stole my family. They nearly killed me, but they didn't succeed. Now I'm hunting them. I'm sure that they're in Wansham at this moment; if not, they've been here recently, and there will be traces to find . . ."

Anita was stunned. Her face had gone pale, her forehead creased with uncertainty, and sympathy. She said, "I'm really sorry. That's awful. I'm really sorry, Dan. I didn't realize it was so serious..."

And that, thought Brady, is that. I may not be the world's most observant man, but this girl knows nothing. But she'll repeat what I said (it didn't take a degree in character interpretation to guess that either) and so the word will be out...

Arachne will come to *me*.

He lifted the bottle of wine and reached across to pour some into Anita's glass. She brightened, the shadow passing from the youthful and erotically pretty features. "I'll help you look. I know lots of people in the village. It's all there is to do, talk, talk, more talk. Maybe someone has seen or heard something. I'll help. What do you say?"

"It's too dangerous..."

"I don't care about that. What's a bit of danger among friends?" The levity was back, and the sparkle in her eyes. She placed her glass down on the bedside table, and gave Brady the sort of look that could not be misinterpreted.

Brady said, "I'd like to know more about the ghosts. If you're psychic to a degree, then yes, perhaps you can help..."

"Let's talk about it," Anita said, "afterwards."

"I'm not so sure that's a good idea."

"Come to bed with me, Dan. Now."

He sipped wine and stared at the girl, aware of her body, of the moisture glistening on her lips. The hunger in him stirred. The thought of her plump, writhing body was too much to cope with. He nodded his head almost imperceptibly. "All right. Let's go to bed."

She stood and raised her blouse above her head, unzipping her mini-skirt and kicking it across the room, where it landed in a heap in the corner. Apart from the belt around her waist which tagged her high, fishnet stockings, she was naked. "I thought you might like a bit of black lace," she said, walking over to Brady and reaching round his neck, so that her breasts touched his face. He grasped her body gently. She was smooth and soft, and she shivered ecstatically at his touch. Kissing her proud nipples, he tasted salt between her breasts. "Take the stockings off," he said, and she obliged and hopped into the bed, pushing back the covers and waiting for him, on her stomach, almost arrogantly positioned to receive him.

Brady stripped and climbed in next to her. "I'm not Clint Eastwood," he said, as she reached for him, and began to passionately kiss his breast and belly.

"Thank God for that."

"Just take it easy. The generation gap . . ."

"I'm going to screw you till you scream. Lie back. I like to go on top."

An hour and a half later Brady had lost contact with his body below the waist, and was beginning to wonder if his heart was about to quit on him. "Enough," he said, breathlessly. Anita was astride him, her hands on his waist supporting herself, and she opened her eyes, stopped her rapid motion, and smiled. "Already?"

"Good God, girl, it's practically tomorrow."

She leaned forward and kissed his nose. "I'm a greedy little bitch."

"I wish there were more of you about. But right now this is one old man who needs to do something normal. Like have a beer."

"You've earned it." She didn't disengage from him, but lay her head across his chest and relaxed. Brady stroked her back, resting his hands on her buttocks. She said, "Can I stay the night?"

"Not a good idea."

"You're right. I wouldn't leave you alone." She looked up at him. "Were you thinking of your wife while we fucked?"

"Some of the time."

Anita considered that. "Would she have minded, do you think?"

"No, I don't think she would. And that," he added quickly, seeing a second question springing to her lips, "is all that I have to say about Alison, okay?"

"Okay." Anita shifted from Brady, and lay next to him, head propped on her hand, watching him.

Brady said, "Tell me about the two freaky ladies."

Anita laughed. She knew the women to whom Brady referred. "Not much to tell, except that they were exactly that. Freaky. Visited the site, talked a lot with my father and Doctor Holbrook. Spent a lot of time exploring the styke with them. Had nothing to say to me, thank God."

"What were their names?"

"Couldn't tell you. I'll ask my father if you like."

"Where did they come from?"

"London, I think. Not sure."

"And where did they go?"

"What is this, Spanish Inquisition time? Where did they go? Couldn't tell you that either. They came together, scared the local supernatural fauna, left separately. One of them, the one wearing all the jewels, must have left a day before the other, the beautiful one. The beautiful one left looking worried. Expect my crippled father had made a pass at her or something."

"What do you mean, scared the local supernatural fauna?"

Anita shifted on the bed, then sat up, looking towards the window and the windy night outside. "That's when I saw the ghost, up on the Roozie. Like a man, like a viking, you know? Long hair, long beard, carrying an axe, walking down the hill towards the beginnings of the styke. Round here, the locals are quite convinced that the excavation has disturbed the dead, but those women did it. Perhaps *they're* this Arachne you're looking for. Maybe they summoned the ghosts of the Roozie. There was no disturbance until they came by. I'm sure of that. I'd only been here for a week, mind you, but the word began to be whispered when they came."

"I want to know more about them," said Brady, reaching to run his hand down the girl's back. She shuddered and made a sound like enjoyment. "Mm. That's nice! I'll ask my father about them, if you like."

"Do that. And keep looking for ghosts. Are there any ghosts in this room? Can you feel a haunting presence?"

Anita glanced round and shook her head. "I don't have that sort of talent. A boyfriend of mine does. He can touch stones and get electric shocks. Walks into a room and hears screams, hundreds of years from the past. Not me. What's that funny smell, by the way?"

"Vinegar. And salt. And various herbs, like garlic."

She looked at him. "Hey, you *are* afraid of ghosts. Garlic stops them doesn't it?"

"It helps. Are you hungry?"
"Starving. Dinner time?"
"I think it must be. I'm feeling quite weak."
Anita giggled.

They ate a substantial dinner in the Royal Oak's extortionately expensive restaurant. Brady paid. Afterwards they went to the bar and sat and talked, idly and tiredly, Brady feeling distinctly weary after the sex and the meal.

They hadn't sat there very long when Brady felt himself grow edgy, restless. The atmosphere in the lounge had changed, becoming almost hostile, almost threatening. It was not something that he could rationally identify. It was not the disapproving gaze of the landlord, Seb Quinn, disgusted by Anita Herbert's displayed legs; nor was it the sombre presence of several locals whose conversation was a classic murmur of the type designed to induce unease in visitors. Brady couldn't think where the change in ambience had come from, but it affected him strongly and it affected Anita, too.

She had gone quite pale, her lips pinched, her gaze darting around the lounge, a sure sign of her own edginess. She was experiencing the presentiment very powerfully, and Brady said, "What is it?"

Shuddering, and reaching for her gin and tonic, Anita shook her head. "I don't know. Like someone's just walked over my grave."

The lounge bar had cooled. No-one else seemed to be restless, or noticeably disturbed. Brady said, "Something's going to happen."

Anita turned wide eyes upon him, her face a mask of concern. "What sort of something?"

It wasn't the same as psychic attack, not the same sense of alertness, followed by a sweaty dizziness, that presaged the targeting of one mind upon another with destructive intent.

It was a premonition. It was something Brady himself had not experienced before, and he was suspicious that both he and Anita were feeling the altered state together. It meant that something in both their lives was registering on them in this peculiar paranormal way.

"Let's walk," said Brady.

"Good idea." She drained her glass and drew her coat around her shoulders. Brady had left his own jacket up in the room.

"I won't be a moment."

He walked quickly upstairs, and along the corridor. As he opened the door to his room, and stepped inside, he switched on the light.

Nothing happened. The bulb was gone. He walked across to the bedside lamp but that too was dead. In the darkness, he stumbled on his case.

And then he heard it...

Breathing.

It was standing by the window, a man-shaped thing, its breathing sounding hoarse and rattly, as if it sucked air through saliva. He caught a glimpse of gleaming eyes, and as his own eyes adjusted to the faint light from outside, he saw that the face was that of a hog, its jowls wet and grinning, the white teeth exposed.

Leaning down towards him, peering at him, piggy eyes bright. He's still alive. What do we do? Kill him, quickly, quickly...

"You!" screamed Brady, and leapt across the bed to the figure, which uttered a throaty, gurgling sound, a chuckle perhaps, or a sound of shock. Brady's hands closed on the warm neck, but he was flung aside against the wall. The creature moved swiftly. Brady could see that it wore a dark leather jacket and tight jeans. Its smell was faint, but unmistakably of urine. As Brady pushed himself away from the wall, with a screech of fury, so he realized that the creature had raised its arms. It was holding a pitchfork, and the weapon was driven at Brady with astonishing power. Brady had just time enough to jerk his head to one side, feeling the left-hand tine cut through the flesh of his neck, which was caught in the fork.

Then the rasping, hollow voice, so familiar to him from that night, four months ago:

"You're a dead man, Brady."

The power of the blow had flung Brady back against the wall, the fork thrusting deeply into the plaster, and wedging Brady's head rigidly. With one hand he worked at the shaft of the implement, the other grabbed at the pig-faced creature, tearing the jacket open as the man tried to run.

Brady's fingers closed on a thin, cold object dangling at the attacker's neck. As the man fled, the amulet ripped away. When Brady freed himself, seconds later, he chased out into the corridor, glanced down and saw the screaming, severed head, carved in stone, that rested in his palm.

It was the one who had been there! The man who had just attacked him had been there, that night! He *had* been one of the Collectors!

Brady raced down the stairs, flinging himself through the lounge bar and out into the high street. He looked each way, frantically, but there was nothing to see.

The man had vanished.

He ran towards the church. He was half aware that somewhere up ahead a woman had screamed. A few moments later, as he rounded the end of the street, he pounded straight into the frantic, hysterical form of a young woman, who beat at his chest, sobbing loudly, and begging him, in broken, almost incomprehensible sentences, to come and help, come and help . . .

TEN

IT HAD BEEN a day of agony for Karen Seymour; not just from the pain in her ravaged body, but from the hurt to her pride, and the clawing pain that grew within her as she thought of her marriage to Jack, and of their son Chris, and of how all of that was threatened, now.

She had limped back to the farmhouse, miserable, weeping, more distressed than she had ever been in her life. She had gone straight to the bathroom, and thoroughly washed her body, horrified at the amount of blood that smeared her limbs. For a second, she felt like screaming, terrified that she might have lost her baby. But she calmed quite quickly, telling herself that she had not experienced the pain of a miscarriage, and nor was there sufficient blood to point to a spontaneous abortion.

She was violently sick, and felt sure that the sound of her retching would wake the Hadlees, but it didn't. She crept back to her room, jumping with fright at every creak of the floorboard, and fetched a blanket. Returning to the bathroom, she locked the door, and slumped down in a corner, huddled inside the wrap, feeling more secure here than she would have in the room she shared with her husband.

She actually slept, waking early in the morning to the sound of the bathroom door being tried. Her heart pounded with shock and she straightened up, wide-eyed, instantly alert. "Who's there?"

"It's Agnes Hadlee. That you, Mrs. Seymour? Are you all right?"

Thank God. What a relief! "I've been sick, that's all. I shan't be long."

"No hurry, dear. I'll be in the kitchen making tea."

Quickly, Karen washed again, freshening her mouth and eyes. Then she cautiously unlocked the door, and tiptoed along the corridor to the guest room at the end. Opening the door, she peered inside, and stood for a moment, uncertain as to what to do.

Jack was sprawled out on the bed, face down, naked. His buttocks were scarred by brambles, the soles of his feet were ragged and torn, the cuts dirt-filled and ugly. He was snoring loudly, his face turned towards Karen, and he had been sick across the sheets. The smell was not strong, but the sight was gut-churning, and Karen gagged as she sat down on the dressing table chair, and stared at her sleeping husband.

He woke slowly, his eyes opening, his body shifting slightly. He made moaning sounds, as if he was dreaming. When he lifted his head, he stared at the clock, then slowly sat up. When he placed his feet on the floor he jerked his legs up, wincing and crying out with pain.

He became aware of Karen, sitting silently in the corner, and when his gaze met hers, there was nothing in his eyes but despair. He shook his head, looking down at his body, touched the lacerations on his skin, then started to shake.

"What happened?" he whispered. "What in God's name happened?"

Karen felt cold, angry. She had been afraid of him, now she saw that he was weak, defenceless. She let her fury rise, express itself in her calmly spoken, ice-cold words. "You raped me."

He wrapped his arms around his chest, hunched forward with a barely audible moan of "God Almighty."

She said, "You raped me. You stripped off my clothes. You bit my breasts. You screwed me like an animal, and against my wishes. I'm hurting, Jack. I'm really, really hurting."

"I know," he said quietly, unable to look at her. "It wasn't me, Kay. I couldn't help it . . ."

"You bastard! Don't make excuses. You brutally attacked me. I ought to kill you. By God, if I thought I could give you any of the pain you gave me, I'd kill you right now! Bastard!" She spat the word at him, her face reddening, the anger beginning to bubble, to become uncontrollable.

Jack looked up at her, his brow furrowed, his eyes expressing the bitter remorse he was feeling. "Kay. It wasn't me. It was as if something took me over. I ran through the fields. My *God*, my feet are hurting. I was tested. I was controlled. I couldn't help what I did . . . I couldn't help it . . ."

She said nothing, watched him, the fury in her face subsiding. He said, "God, Kay, I'm sorry. I'm sorry for what I did to you. God I'm sorry. I'll do anything . . . anything . . . I'm lost, Kay."

"What does that mean? Lost where? Lost from what? Lost from me? Damn right. I'm going home, Jack. I'm packing my things and going home, and when I get to Edmonton, I'm taking Christopher, and beginning divorce proceedings." The words came out like gunfire, cold, clear, determined, and yet behind them the mind that caused them to be spoken was not sure. Jack was not normal, he was not right. He had been obsessed with Wansham and now he was muttering about being possessed by something that had made him accede to its will. Perhaps he was mad. Perhaps it was illness. Perhaps he was right.

Whatever the case, he clearly needed help.

He said, "Please don't. God Karen, don't leave me. Not now, I need you. I'm terrified. I'm going to be killed, I know it. I know I am. I need help . . ."

The word "killed" sent a shockwave through Karen, and all her anger began to dissipate. She stared at her distraught husband, and somehow the pain in her body went away and she saw the pain in his, and the terrible shadow in his mind.

"What do you mean?"

"I'm going to be killed," he said. "They've called me here. They want me back . . . they have to kill me . . ."

"Who does? Who wants to kill you? Who's called you back?"

"I don't know," he said feebly, his head shaking. "The one who lives here. An old man, centuries old. A ghost, something like a ghost. It wants me, it's going to kill me. I'm strong, and it needs my strength, and it's going to drain it from me . . . Oh God, Karen. Get me away from here. Please. Help me."

She helped him. But in the first instance, it was help to cleanse the deep gashes on his body. She bathed his feet, wrapped them in bandages. The cuts on his body were more grazes than anything, and she dabbed iodine onto them, covering the more ragged gashes with plaster.

Jack dressed, but refused breakfast. Karen was hungry, and she went down to kippers and toast that Mrs. Hadlee had prepared. Jack was ill, she explained. They'd be going home later that day. Yes, it was a shame when they'd made all that effort to get here. Never mind, there would be other times.

But when she went back up to the room, she found Jack sitting by the window, staring out across the farmland. He was brighter, now, and the mood of despair had passed.

"How are you?" Karen asked, and he said, "Stronger." He reached for her hand, and tugged her to him. Tears welled up in his eyes and he almost choked as he said, "Kay . . . last night . . . I'm terrified. I'm so sorry . . . God, when I think what I did . . ."

She squeezed him tighter. "Forget it."

Forget it! What empty words! She would never forget that assault, even if she could forgive it.

"Something is happening to me, Kay . . ."

"I know."

"Something bad. Something evil." He was shaking, the tears rolling freely down his cheeks. "A part of me isn't *me*. Last summer . . ."

"What about last summer?" she prompted when he trailed off.

"I was walking out across the styke," he said. "You had period pains, remember? You stayed back. I went out along the country road, and walked across the peat bog, towards the ridge."

"I remember."

"I saw a ghost. It was the ghost of a man, quite tall, very muscular. Long hair, long beard, and it was running towards me. I didn't realize it was a ghost until it hit me, and there was no pain. I wasn't bowled over. The apparition just passed through me, and vanished. But I was sick and disoriented for hours afterwards. I reckon I'd been walking at about eleven in the morning. Moments later it was four in the afternoon. That's when I fell in the pond. Afterwards, I thought I must have dreamed it . . ."

"You never told me this."

"I know I didn't. I didn't think you'd believe me. I felt reluctant to tell you. I didn't want you doubting me, because I was already doubting myself."

Karen leaned down to kiss the top of his head. His grip on her hand was tighter, almost desperate. What was it that he believed? That a ghost he had crossed, out on the bog, had called him back, and had indicated that it would kill him? Was he attributing everything that was happening to him to that strange encounter, dream though it almost certainly had been?

"Listen," she said. "Jack, we've put this off for long enough . . ."

"What have we put off?"

"A doctor," she said gently. "It's time to take you to see a man whose experience might guide us. You're right: it wasn't you last night, attacking me. My Jack doesn't force himself brutally on women; my Jack doesn't force himself enough in my opinion; my Jack certainly doesn't screw his wife in a barn, acting like an animal. Whatever's happening to you, my darling, it's mental, it has to be faced, it has to be tackled. And I'll support you, you know I will."

His grip on her hand was convulsively tight. "I'm frightened, Kay," he said. "I'm really frightened."

"I know you are," she whispered. "But there really is *nothing* to fear. We'll get you to a consultant. We'll go to London, and see a specialist."

Karen wanted to leave immediately, but she wasn't going to force Jack to leave until he was fully ready. He seemed undecided, torn between staying in a place that terrified him and leaving a place which had such a hold over him.

They ate lunch together in the room, then packed their cases again. Jack wanted to walk to the sea, and they cut across the farm and up onto the sea-bluff, walking for over an hour. It was a blustery day, and Karen was chilled to the marrow, but she kept walking until Jack indicated that it was time to return to the farm. They found the road, and began strolling the shorter distance home.

They had not walked more than half a mile when they heard the sound of a car behind them. The road was narrow, and to be on the safe side, they stood at the road's edge, and watched the vehicle approach.

It was a landrover, and Karen recognized it as that belonging to the archaeologists up on the ridge.

The man driving it was young, and she didn't recognize him; but the older man in the passenger seat was the bespectacled doctor whom she believed was called Holbrook. It had been him who had acknowledged her yesterday.

The vehicle stopped and Holbrook leaned out of his window. "I thought I recognized you."

"Yes. Hello. How's the digging?"

"Dirty work," said Holbrook, and smiled at Jack. "Are you going to the farm? Can we offer you a lift?"

"Yes *please*," said Karen, delighted at the chance of getting out of the cold, miserable wind. Jack said nothing. Karen thought he seemed uneasy at the idea of riding with the two men, but he climbed into the back seat anyway, and the landrover lurched off down the road.

Little was said in the few minutes it took to return to Kett's Farm. Holbrook was surprised to hear that they were leaving so soon after arriving for their vacation. "We thought we might have seen you up at Uffricshame. On the ridge, I mean. You'd be more than welcome."

"Thank you," said Karen. "But it doesn't look as if we'll have time now."

"Never mind," said Holbrook. "Not the most visually exciting of sites that I've worked on. But it's always good to have a visitor or two. Breaks the monotony."

"I'll walk up later," said Jack, and Karen glanced at him, puzzled and slightly startled.

"More than welcome," said Holbrook.

"I thought we had to get away," Karen said quietly, and when Jack looked at her his eyes were cold, his lips pressed tightly together. It seemed to Karen that he was restraining either anger or impatience. He just said, "We'll leave tomorrow. One more night seems like a good idea to me."

"Jack . . . !" she began, but the harshness of his gaze caused the words to dry up on her lips. She felt a bitter, painful chill, a response to the fact that she had recognized the return of the obsessed man. This was the part-Jack man again, the semi-beast who had attacked her the night before, and who seemed to control so easily the gentle man that she had married.

The landrover stopped at the farm to let them off, then lurched along the rough track and up to the ridge. Jack watched it go, almost thoughtfully. Karen tugged at his sleeve. "Let's go in, Jack."

He followed her silently up to the room. Their bags were packed. They were ready to leave. Karen said, "Now, Jack. Let's go now . . ."

He peered through the window and said, quite sharply, "I can't."

"You can. Let's *go*."

"I must stay. Just one more night. We'll go tomorrow." He turned back to the room, and walked round the bed, taking her hands in his. The expression on his face was one of worry, masked by a certain coldness. "One more night," said the cold part of him, and the frightened part broke through, his eyes narrowing, his brow furrowing. "Don't let me out of your sight, Kay. Stay with me, whatever happens . . ."

She squeezed his hands. "Whatever happens," she echoed. "If you're frightened, Jack, perhaps we should move to the hotel in the town, be around people. Shall I get the police out here?"

"No," he said sharply. "Not necessary. Just . . . stay around me."

She sat down on the bed, watching him. Later, she fetched tea and sandwiches from Mrs. Hadlee, and they sat and ate in silence in the room; Karen read a magazine. Jack stared moodily at her, occasionally pacing up and down the room, increasingly restless.

After dinner, which was conducted in silence, to the embarrassment of the Hadlees who could tell that there was something very wrong, Jack took a bath, lingering in the water for nearly an hour. He kept the door open, and Karen checked in on him regularly. When he asked for his clothes, she brought them, and helped him dry his back. He seemed quite cheerful, far more relaxed than earlier, and although he was still ashamed for his unprecedented attack on her the night before, he made a playful pass. She responded tensely, sinking into his bear hug, letting him kiss her, but keeping her hands between their bodies.

But she was delighted. It was good to feel the old Jack, the father of their son, the loving husband.

"I need a drink," he said, walking out of the bathroom naked, the towel flung round his neck.

"Jack! What would Mrs. Hadlee say . . ."

He grinned and glanced back at her. "Shall I go and ask her?"

"Put some clothes on!" She could imagine the response from the straight-laced farmer's wife. And she didn't imagine Farmer Hadlee himself would be too pleased to have a naked man walking about on his landing.

Karen popped down to the kitchen, to ask for two glasses of scotch, which Mrs. Hadlee was delighted to supply. "Feeling better, is he?" she asked, and Karen was able to take the opportunity to apologize for the atmosphere at dinner.

"We'll be leaving in the morning. Jack really is rather ill."

"Don't worry, my dear. There'll be other years."

Karen took the drinks up to their room. "I think we'll get a refund, if we play our cards right . . ." she said as she stepped inside. The bedroom was empty. Glancing back at the bathroom she could see that that, too, was deserted. "Jack? Where are you?"

Oh, God no!

Her heart missed a beat, and she felt violently sick for a second. The next moment she had placed the glasses on the dresser, turned, and fled down the stairs.

She ran to the front door, which was open. Out in the night the wind was sharp and cold, and in the distance she could see Jack, running towards the sea-bluff, wearing just his shirt and jeans.

She shouted after him, but he didn't stop.

Karen gave chase, stumbling twice on the rough track, and cutting her knee open. Her plaintive cry of pain and despair would have carried easily to Jack's hearing, but he kept running, ignoring the calling voice behind him.

Karen limped on, desperately trying to keep her husband's speeding figure in view. He raced along the road, not cutting across the boggy land up to the sea's edge, and she was glad of that.

Twenty minutes later she was exhausted, frozen, and the blood from her cut knee had pooled in her right shoe and made walking both difficult and uncomfortable. In the windy darkness she stopped and looked about the blasted landscape, across the flat, moonlit fields, through the waving forms of trees, that seemed to reach up all around her, making it hard for her to see anything. She was close to the town, and she could see the dark, unwelcoming walls of the church nearby. From that direction came the murmur of voices, and she crossed the stile into the churchyard, picking her way carefully between the rough-edged tombstones until she could see Jack again.

"Jack . . ." she said, and walked towards him, frowning, trying to see who it was that he was addressing.

Then she saw. He was standing slightly in the lee of the church, and only his stick gave him away. She could see the glimmer of moon on his teeth and eyes. Doctor Herbert. Jack was standing, facing him. Karen stepped forward and heard the words.

"You are the last," this from Doctor Herbert, who stepped out from the dark, so that Karen could see he wore a dark shirt and flannel trousers, the shirt open at the neck. The wind blew his clothes, and he ought to have been freezing. He was holding something in his hand, out of her sight.

Jack said, "I've come a long way."

"You've come the longest, and you are the most important."

"Who called me?"

Herbert laughed. "Why Jack, who do you think? I called you. You are the last, you are the strongest."

"Where are the others?"

"In the bogs. One lies below us, in the crypt. They came quickly, and my strength has grown. But you are the strongest, and I need you more than the others."

Karen was dazzled, bemused by the words. She limped towards her husband and called "Jack! What are you doing, Jack?"

Herbert looked towards her, but he smiled, looked back at the man before him. Jack Seymour, without looking round, shouted, "Go back to the farm, Karen. Go back. Go home!"

"No! What's going on? Tell me what's going on!"

She hesitated just briefly, then realized what it was that Herbert was holding, for he had lifted his right arm slightly. Moonlight gleamed on the axe blade.

"My God. No!" she screamed, and ran to her husband, but Jack swung round with his fist, and the blow to her face was stunning, agonizing, paralysing . . .

She was flung back, striking her head against a stone as she fell. Dazed, too weak to move, she watched the nightmare act above her, struggling to speak, desperate to scream a warning, to stop what was happening.

Jack stepped towards Herbert, who raised the axe.

"The others panicked. They tried to break way," said Herbert. "At the last moment their reason prevailed. But it did them no good. Their bodies lie lifeless below the ground, and what they stole resides in me . . . The spirit is almost complete . . ."

"I am the strongest," said Jack. "I have waited for this moment."

"Jack, for Christ's sake, run!" screamed Karen, struggling to sit up, finding her head shooting with pain, stumbling and staggering to her feet. "He's going to kill you! Jack, he's going to kill you!"

The axe raised into the air, the iron blade bright. It was a viking axe, double-bladed, swift and manipulable; a deadly weapon, to be wielded by a deadly man . . .

"Jack! For Christ's sake, he's going to kill you!"

But Herbert passed the axe to Jack Seymour. Seymour grasped the weapon and as Karen watched, horrified, stunned, he swung it once, twice through the air, getting the feel of the weapon, listening to the sound it made as it sliced through the night . . .

And suddenly Doctor Herbert cried out, backing away slightly. "No! Not like this! This isn't the way . . . no! No!"

His final scream was cut short as Jack brought the larger blade smashing down through Herbert's skull, splitting the bone to the neck, spilling blood and brains across the graveyard as he wrenched the axe free.

Karen watched, paralysed with shock and fear, as her husband stood above the body and used the axe to split the breast bone of the dead man, wrenching the ribs into a broken cage, spreading the lungs into eagle's wings . . .

When Karen found her voice, it was simply to scream. She fled from the churchyard, sobbing with hysteria, only half aware of the triumphant yelling of the man behind her.

Her husband, Jack Seymour. A man totally possessed by evil, and now totally beyond her ability to help.

Eleven

"CLOSE THE DOOR," said Brady, as he helped Karen Seymour into the lounge bar of the Royal Oak. "And lock up!" He addressed the comment to the landlord, and Quinn, obeying the authority in Brady's voice, despite his confusion, walked quickly to the double doors and bolted them.

"What's going on?" Quinn asked as he came back across to the bar and stared at the dishevelled, distressed figure of Karen Seymour. Brady had set the weeping woman down on a bar stool and was inspecting the cut on her knee. Anita Herbert fussed about, asked, "*Who's* been killed?"

"Killed?" echoed Quinn, and Brady said, "Up by the church. There's been a murder. No. Wait . . ." Quinn had been moving towards the phone. "Not yet, if that's the police you're thinking of calling. Not yet."

Quinn's round face hardened. He was no fool, and there was something amiss if a stranger told him so curtly not to get the police along to the scene of a killing. "Why not?"

"Just wait . . ." said Brady, adding, "do you have a gun?"

"Aye. A shotgun. And an old army revolver."

"Get them," said Brady, and Karen Seymour started to cry again.

"Don't hurt him," she begged, and her hands closed on Brady's arms like vices. He stared at her tear-stained features, eye make-up streaking her cheeks, dirt smearing her skin.

"Protection only," Brady said. "Tell me what happened . . ."

"He's possessed," sobbed Karen, her head shaking with despair. "It's not Jack at all, it's something else. We've got to help him. We've got to *help* him. Don't kill him, for God's sake don't shoot him."

"*Who's* been killed?" Anita Herbert asked again, and Brady snapped, "I don't know yet. I haven't been up to the church."

A voice he recognized as Alan Keeton's said, "I'll come with you, man. I'm pretty good with my feet if we get attacked."

Keeton had just appeared from the stairs to the landing where the guest rooms were situated. His mother was in bed. The youngster's face was alive with interest, almost excitement, at the thought of a break in the dull routine of supporting his mother through her crisis.

Quinn reappeared with a bowl of hot water, soap and a flannel. Anita Herbert took charge of cleaning Karen Seymour's deep knee cut. Quinn, out of sight of the shaking woman, indicated the shotgun and pistol.

As best she could, Karen explained what had happened. Brady listened, intrigued. The obsession with Wansham, the return to England under circumstances more suggestive of a man being lost than a holiday being gained, the restless, distracted behaviour of Jack Seymour, his sense of being two people, and one of them growing in strength. She hesitated, uncertainly, then described the rape, and the way Jack's body had seemed ghost-like, hideous. And then the murder.

He had been summoned, she was sure of that. He had known he was to be killed, and yet he had gone along quite willingly to the church, for a rendezvous with the man who would slaughter him. And instead of Jack being axed to death, the man had given the axe to her husband, and he had committed the most terrible murder before her eyes.

He had chased her, but given up after a few yards, and run screeching—as if in triumph—off towards the farmland.

"Who did he kill?" Brady asked. "Did you recognize the man?"

Karen nodded. "I think so. He was the old man with the stick, from the excavations. Doctor Herbert . . ."

"My father!" Anita screamed, and for a moment it seemed

as if all hell had broken loose. She had run to the main doors of the hotel and was almost ripping the bolts open, her voice a shrill screech of shock and horror. Alan Keeton ran to her, pulled her from the door and fought to calm her down as she scratched and beat at his face.

Karen Seymour watched, open-mouthed, stunned, all tears suddenly stifled. "What have I done?" she whispered, and Brady squeezed her shoulder. "You weren't to know," he said.

Anita Herbert began to cry, and through her tears her voice was like that of a little girl. "I must go out there. He's my father, I must see him..."

Brady said to Karen Seymour, "Look after her if you can. I take it that Jack is dangerous..."

Karen's lower lip quivered, and tears welled up in her eyes. Brady mentally kicked himself, realizing that he couldn't expect one distraught woman to look after another. He used the phone behind the bar to call Agnes Hadlee from Kett's Farm, doing so on Quinn's advice, Quinn's own wife, Mavis, being away for the evening.

When Mrs. Hadlee arrived she took charge immediately, marching the two younger women into the kitchen where, no doubt, she would make strong coffee for them all.

Anita Herbert went reluctantly. Her last cry, back to Brady, was, "I want to see him. I want to *see* him!"

"Keep the doors and windows closed and locked," Brady said to Mrs. Hadlee. "On no account let Jack Seymour into the premises..."

She looked shocked, but nodded her head, accepting unquestioningly the voice of authority. "Very well. You be careful, Mister Brady."

"We'll all be careful."

He, Quinn and Alan Keeton stepped out into the night. Brady carried the army pistol, Quinn the shotgun; Keeton went unarmed, but picked up a long, heavy piece of wood as they crossed the gate into the churchyard. The night was cold, and all of a sudden seemed unnaturally still. They could hear the crash of the sea against the shore, and the distant winds out across the styke. Eyes alert for the darting shape of Jack Seymour, they walked around the church, and soon found the grisly remains of Doctor Herbert.

"Good God, man," said Alan Keeton, his face looking pale and sickly in the partial moonlight. Quinn, despite his tough constitution, was sick over against the wall of the church.

"My Lord," he said, wiping his mouth with a handkerchief. "I don't think I've ever seen anything so cruel."

Brady felt sick too. He noticed that Herbert's hands were clenched, the mouth opened in a silent scream, the eyes stretched wide, and still staring blindly at the sky. The stink from the corpse was abominable. He briefly memorized the way the lungs had been spread, and the ribs cracked and made to stand on end. He was powerfully reminded of the Ripper murders, with their ritual display of organs, a reflection of Masonic ritual killings. But this was not the same. It was ritual, but not Masonic. Brady memorized the details, intending to find out what the peculiar display really meant.

What else had Karen Seymour heard? *There's one below, in the crypt. Others in the bogs.* He said to Quinn, "Fetch the vicar. We need to get into the church."

Quinn frowned. "Harry White won't like that. He's always in bed by eight."

"Get him out of bed. It's urgent. And bring the keys to the crypt."

As Quinn vanished into the gloom, Keeton said, "What's in the crypt?"

"Another body. I'm sure of it."

"Oh God. My father . . ." the youth had closed his eyes and started to shake. Brady squeezed his arm.

"I'm sorry, Alan. It may *not* be your father, but I'm sure your father's dead."

"Then where . . . ?"

"In the bog, I expect." He was too cold, too frightened, too confused to be anything but cruel. He would have liked to pick his words more carefully, but it seemed suddenly, and callously, quite pointless to do so. Jack Seymour had been called back to Wansham to fulfill a destiny that had involved his killing of Herbert. From what Karen had heard, Seymour was "the strongest," and whatever had possessed Seymour in part now possessed him in full, using his young, strong body, abandoning Herbert's crippled, ageing one, something that Herbert had not expected.

Others had been called back. Keeton and Shackleford, perhaps others still. Their fate was certain. If Seymour had carried a part of some possessing spirit, then so had they: called back to return that spirit to its source. And the return had involved their violent killing, and Angela Huxley had been aware of it, on the plane of her Hinterland.

When the Vicar arrived with the key to the crypt, grumbling and cold, but too old, too sleepy to make any real objection, Brady led the way into the church, and down the steps behind the font. He opened the heavy oak door to the vault and switched on the electric light. The place was musty, damp-smelling, and there was that other smell with which he was well familiar: the acrid, offensive stink of blood.

He walked around the skull-lined walls and soon saw the sprawled body lying behind a central stone coffin. The man's head had been severed between upper and lower jaw.

To his disgust, Brady suddenly realized that the staring cranial portion of the head had been stuck between two skulls on the shelves.

"It's Shackleford," Quinn said, peering at the gruesome trophy. "He arrived alone, brought back to the town on the same impulse. Poor bugger. Who did this to him; Seymour?"

"Herbert," said Brady. "I can't be sure, but it's the best answer I have."

Harry White was agog and aghast with what had been discovered in the crypt of his church. Quinn calmed him down, led him back upstairs, reassuring him that there wasn't a witchcraft practice in the area, and that the police would be told soon enough. Alan Keeton, his long hair hanging free, his eyes sad and narrowed behind his round-framed glasses, reached out to touch the head on the shelves.

"Then my father's body is in the mud. Probably where my mother last saw him. Man, that's horrible. Horrible."

"I'm sorry," said Brady.

"Herbert called him. Is that what you're saying?"

"The spirit that possessed Herbert. Last summer, when there was a certain activity in the area . . ." *they are awaken-*

ing. They are reaching. They are awakening . . . "I imagine that several partial possessions occurred. A ghost was being raised . . . maybe. I don't know how."

"But you think my father was one of those . . . partially taken over?"

"Yes. I'm sure of it. The full awakening occurred later. The group that I'm pursuing have been working in this area, and I'm sure it was they who organized the resurrection of the ghost. It inhabited Herbert, but was incomplete . . ."

"And in a frail, ageing body."

Brady nodded thoughtfully. "Karen said that Herbert's last words were, 'No, this isn't the way. Not like this.' Or something to that effect."

Keeton understood. "Taken by surprise you mean. He hadn't expected to be a sacrifice himself."

Brady's eyes glowed with comprehension. He almost smiled, staring at the baffled youngster, but not really seeing him. "It's gone wrong," he said. "Of course. Arachne *was* here. They've raised the ghost of the local chieftain, Uffric. The spirit must have power, shamanic power, perhaps. And a talisman." He was remembering the Stoneface's words through Angela Huxley: *the stone of power. They must not find it.* "Arachne wanted that power, and they've raised the spectre. But it's gone wrong. The ghost has taken control. It was betrayed, remember the legend? Betrayed by the woman he loved, and killed, and now it wants revenge!" He laughed. "Arachne aren't quite as powerful as they thought. Herbert has been killed." He reached into his pocket and drew out the amulet of the severed, screaming head. "There's at least one other, probably two, still in the area. And the one who wore this can't attack with his mind."

Keeton reached out for the amulet and stared at it, his face grimacing at the screaming head, carved in stone. "I've seen this before. Not an amulet, a drawing. My father drew it . . ." He met Brady's gaze. "He drew it several times, as if he was obsessed by it."

"I've seen it too," said Brady quietly. "It's a copy, I think, of a more ancient talisman, a stone of power, buried somewhere nearby. Arachne are seeking it. The man who attacked me just now was wearing it, and he had visited me once before. The voice was the same. He couldn't kill then, he wasn't 'allowed' to. But he can kill now. But he was too quick, too panicked," he tugged down his shirt collar, and Keeton winced at the raw wound across Brady's neck. In the heat of the chase, and the meeting with Karen Seymour, the throbbing pain had gone unnoticed.

"They know you're here, then."

"Yes. And they know I'm hunting them. If only I could be *sure* . . ."

Keeton frowned, his attention half on the grisly spectacle of the dead man. "Sure about what?"

Brady glanced at him. "About who they are. It's not just their deaths I want, it's information. Where is my family? Where have they been taken? And I can't just confront a stranger, on the off-chance that because he worked with a member of the secret order that he's one too . . ."

Keeton understood. "The men on the ridge, the archaeologists. But the crazy girl was up there too. Anita . . ."

"I know," said Brady quietly. "I know that very well indeed."

If Keeton had been about to say more, he was prevented by the breathless arrival of Quinn at the bottom of the vault stairs. "We've got trouble," he said. "You'd better come and sort her out."

Brady climbed the stone steps back to the church, and could hear the sounds of shock and nausea from the girl before he had left the cold interior of the building. Anita was leaning against the wall, hands on her knees, face drawn and peculiarly twisted in the half-light as she looked at the remains of her father. She had been sick, and the liquid had splashed her dress. She was sweating profusely, perhaps from shock, perhaps from running, after she had escaped Agnes Hadlee's watchful eye in the hotel.

Brady reached out for her arm. "Go back to the Oak, Anita. Go back now. We'll take care of this."

She shook his touch from her body, glared at him. "Find the bastard who did this! Don't just stand there gaping. Find him! And get the police. God . . . oh *God*, look at him!" Disgust touched her features. "No man deserves to die so horribly. My poor father . . ." Again the intense, angry gaze on

Brady. "I don't care if his wife is carrying triplets! I don't *care*, Brady. Find him and blow his fucking brains out. *I* will!" She made a grab for the shotgun that Quinn was holding, but Brady's grip wrested her fingers from the weapon, and he dragged her back against the church wall.

"We'll find him, Anita! We have to, for all our sakes. For safety's sake. But believe me, Jack Seymour is possessed. Killing him might set that spirit free. It might take anyone. We have to capture him! First we have to take him alive!"

Anita was still shaking, with rage Brady imagined, and with repressed grief. For all that she had said about her father, her irritation with him had merely masked love, not obliterated it. Watching her, tapping into her fury, he could hardly bring himself to believe that she was in any way involved with Arachne.

She had whispered something, then closed her eyes in bitter anguish. Brady said, "What was that? Eagle?"

She repeated, "Blood eagle." Her eyes opened again, and she pushed herself away from the wall, looking down at her dress.

"What's a blood eagle?" Brady asked curiously, noticing that Quinn was slowly shaking his head, also watching the girl. The vicar stood, grim and silent, some way from the group.

Anita stabbed a finger at her father's body and angrily snapped, "*That's* a blood eagle! That mess! My father. God, what do you want, a fucking lecture? My father has been murdered. We ought to get the police. Don't stand there asking fucking stupid questions . . ." Her anger gave way to tears again. Brady reached for her and she leaned against him, sobbing and shaking, clutching at his shoulders with hands whose nails were torn and split and badly bleeding. He couldn't imagine how she had managed to damage herself so much.

He made soothing sounds, and after a moment she stopped crying so bitterly, merely stared at him with the tears streaming from her eyes and making the dirt on her face run and smear.

"Ritual murder," Brady whispered. "Is that what you're saying? You must tell me, Anita, because we have to find the killer, and everything we know about him, and what he has done, will help us."

She accepted that, nodded, and rested her hands against Brady's chest. She seemed so lost, so young, compared to the voracious and experienced woman of scant hours before. She eventually looked back at the corpse, and her lips quivered as she spoke. "The lungs spread out like eagle's wings, through the ribs, made to stand up like feathers . . . Christ!" The fact of describing the horrendous savaging of her father's body made her gorge rise again, and for a moment Brady thought she would be sick; but she kept control, swallowed hard, and wept for a moment. "It's viking," she finally said. "An honoured death, sacrificed to Odin. The invading vikings practiced it on the Kings of East Anglia especially. It was an honoured way to die . . . although the sacrificial victim didn't think so. It's sick, really sick to kill like that. He must be really sick . . ."

"He's possessed," Brady whispered, reminding Anita for what seemed like the hundredth time, trying to drive the point home. "He's possessed by something that lived over a thousand years ago. Uffric! The spirit that died at the hands of vikings, perhaps died by the blood eagle. It's revenge that motivates it now. Killing in the way that *it* was killed. Jack Seymour is the vehicle of that revenge, the solid flesh that wields the axe. It's his passenger that we must exorcise. It's his passenger that killed your father, after your father had helped tto resurrect that spirit."

And very softly, very sadly, Anita said, "I know. I know that's true. Get me out of here, Dan. Please. Now."

They returned quickly, edgily, to the Royal Oak hotel, entered the premises and bolted and barred the doors. While Brady and Quinn had been up at the church, Agnes Hadlee had called five local men and primed them for what was to come. Mrs. Quinn had returned as well. Brady explained the nature of Jack Seymour, and what he believed to be happening in the village, and after the initial shocked disbelief, the five divided up the town and surrounding area and began the daunting task of speaking to every household, warning them to stay in, to stay locked up, and on no account to call the police as yet. The Royal Oak became the headquarters for the operation, and Quinn and his wife stood by the phone, in case anyone should call through that they had seen Seymour.

Brady felt that it was too much to expect *no-one* to contact the police, but the insular nature of the small town, the liking among the people for handling their own affairs, would perhaps give him a few hours to play with.

At dawn they would begin the hunt, from the sea to the styke, and through every farm between. First, though, Brady had a visit to make, an encounter that was not unlike walking into the lion's den.

As he made ready to leave the Oak and go to his car, Anita Herbert came up to him. She looked almost deathly pale, at the end of her tether, desperately tired. "I want to go back to the house," she said, and Brady frowned.

"Why? It's not safe, you know that!"

"Why shouldn't it be safe? Ewen Holbrook and Simon Moss are there. I need to change, to wash, to think about going back to London. Take me to the house, Dan. Please."

"All right. That's where I was going anyway."

"To tell Doctor Holbrook?"

"Yes. In part."

She didn't take it any further, just nodded her head and waited quietly by the double doors. Shock had taken her over, drying her tears, making her seem almost hard. Brady went behind the bar and into the kitchen, where Karen Seymour was sitting silently, almost numbed with the horror of what she was experiencing. She had listened to Brady's instructions to the villagers, and heard him repeatedly emphasize that Jack should be taken alive, and not killed. She had come to trust Dan Brady, even though just an hour before he had been a total stranger. So when Brady came into the kitchen she managed a smile, and reached out to take his hand.

"I'm coming with you," she said.

Brady shook his head. "Stay here. Stay safe. I'm going to a place to which Jack may be heading . . ."

"Don't hurt him," she begged, and Brady squeezed her hand.

"I need Jack in my way almost as much as you need him in yours. I can't do more than emphasize to people to take care, and to try to preserve his life. *I'll* certainly be preserving his life. Don't leave the Oak, Karen. Stay inside, stay in company, and if it all gets too much for you, have a weep, a shout, beat

Quinn . . . he's quite used to it. *Use* people. Don't go out on your own."

As Brady moved to stand, Karen's fingers closed tightly on his wrists, and her stare took on an intensity that suggested fear to the man. She said, "Am I in danger? From Jack?"

Brady saw no reason not to say exactly what was on his mind. "Yes, I believe you are. There's a local legend about Uffric that I believe has to be taken seriously. He was betrayed by a woman, his wife. It's Uffric's spirit that is possessing Jack, of that I'm quite sure. It's a spirit in passionate search for revenge, and you—the wife of the vessel that carries the spirit—have to be considered a target for that revenge." Her expression never changed; she watched him with wide-eyes understanding, and deep-rooted horror.

"Jack is coming for me, coming to kill me. The rape was just the beginning. There is murder to follow . . ."

"It won't happen," Brady said. "We'll find him, and exorcise him . . ."

"How? How will you do that?"

"I know the way," Brady said, and crossed the fingers of his right hand, praying that the lie, as it stood, would soon become less of a lie. It *had* to be possible to release body and spirit from the haunted man. Only a few weeks before, days after he had left hospital, a similar release had happened to him, part of his own spirit returning from the house that had trapped it. It was just a question of finding out how to do it. That was all. Simple. "I know the way," he repeated. "You just look after yourself, and resist any and all temptation to go searching for Jack on your own."

Minutes later, Brady and Anita Herbert left the Royal Oak, and drove in Brady's car out of the village, into the dark, silent night, towards the house on the Little Minster road, which the archaeologists had used as their base. The army pistol sat heavy and comforting in Brady's jacket pocket. It was not Holbrook that worried him so much as the younger member of the team, Simon Moss. Moss was sullen and sour-faced, and had hardly spoken a word when Brady had briefly visited the Roozie site the day before; but his height was right, and his weight was right, and his menace was right . . . for the man who had attacked him in his room that evening. He was strong, then, and he was potentially dangerous—assuming that he *was* part of Arachne.

It was almost unbearably frustrating for Brady to feel himself so close, and yet to be filled with doubt. A confrontation was needed as much for his own satisfaction as for any reasonable hope that he might penetrate one or two of Arachne's masks. Without proof, without certainty, he had only intuition and luck to fall back on.

The house was in darkness as he swung the car into the narrow drive at the front. The door was locked. Anita fumbled for her key in her bag, and led the way inside. The place was totally deserted, and although she and Brady walked into every room, it was clear that the house had been vacated for some hours. Holbrook's clothes were still in evidence, but Moss's small alarm clock was not.

Brady imagined that they had taken certain essentials and moved base. Anita was as puzzled by the absence of her two colleagues, but put it down to their having returned to London, perhaps overnight; it was something that was part of the usual routine. They might even have gone off to see the local Supervisor of sites, to whom they were required to make regular reports.

As Anita stripped for her bath, Brady searched the house thoroughly. When he could hear splashing in the lukewarm water, he moved quickly to her father's room and searched through Herbert's several jackets and suitcase. He found nothing. He checked in on Anita, who lay quite still in the water, staring into space; Brady could see that she had been weeping. "Are you going to be all right?"

She shook her head very slowly, not looking at him. "I feel sick. For the life of me I don't know what to do, now. I can't get him out of my mind . . ." Her eyes screwed up and she began to rack with sobs, raising a hand to her face to try and stifle the sound of her distress.

Brady withdrew from the cold bathroom and went back to the room which Herbert had occupied, seeking under the bed, in drawers, tapping the wall softly in an attempt to locate hidden cubbyholes. He didn't know what he was looking for, and could see no reason why Herbert should have carried evidence of Arachne with him wherever he went. But an impulse kept

Brady searching, and he turned his attention to the leather suitcase again.

This time he found it. It was as if it had been calling to him, his daughter's voice transmitting through the crumpled paper, the scrawled, untidy words.

In a sealed compartment, in which only thin sheets of paper would be concealed, Brady found three notes, addressed to Herbert, and signed simply G.

Heart pounding, he read and re-read the shortest:

The Brady girl's talents are unusual. We can use her before Roundelay. Tell the Mammath.

The Brady girl! Marianna!

She had been alive when this note was written, alive and noticed, her slight psychic talents of interest to the group who had stolen her. But what was "Roundelay?" And why did it sound so final to Brady? So terribly final . . .

Brady sat on the bed and his hand shook as he held the note, and stared at it. What had happened to the other two, Alison and Dominick? Had they been separated? Would Roundelay be as final for them as he sensed it would be for Marianna?

The tension that he felt building within him had to be shaken off. He heard Anita splashing noisily in the bath, as if she were climbing out. He glanced swiftly at the other two notes, recognizing only the name "Magondathog" . . .

Go on to Magondathog as soon as possible. The power at the source is developing and must be awakened soon.

The other read simply, *The mind Wickhurst is dead. Tell the Mammath.*

Brady tucked the notes into his pocket, closing the case. Wickhurst, he thought, and substituted "Campbell." The secret name for the man he had killed.

Who, or what, was the Mammath?

Anita appeared in the doorway, wet and dripping, a towel draped around her above her breasts, covering her quite inadequately. "I want to stay here," she said. "I need to think."

"I won't allow it," said Brady. "Get your clothes, your things, and I'll take you back to the hotel."

"I don't want to go back," she retorted feebly, sadly. "I'll wait for Ewen and Simon. I'll tell them what's happened."

Brady rose from the bed, picked up Herbert's case and carried it with him as he crossed the room and took Anita's cold, damp arm, guiding her gently to her own room. He flung the case onto the bed. "Pack your things."

"I'm staying, Dan! You're not my father. I'm staying here." Almost sullenly. "I need to think."

"Pack," Brady said. "If I have to drag you back to the hotel screaming, then I'll do it. Jack Seymour isn't playing games, and part of what has inhabited him might be . . ." He broke off as the cruelty of what he was saying struck him, but he could see no way round facing the truth. "Part of him may be your father, and your father's memories might bring Seymour to this house, to hide, perhaps, to lie low until he can strike again. I don't think you should be here to meet him."

Anita was looking horrified. "My father's mind . . . in him? In the man that killed him? It's not possible!"

"He's possessed. Get your clothes on. Hurry, I want to get back."

And silently, then, her mind clearly on thoughts of her father and the evil thing that had happened to him, Anita Herbert gathered her clothes together, and more sensibly clad in jeans and a thick Shetland wool jumper, accompanied Brady back to the car, back to Wansham.

Karen Seymour had calmed down considerably. She sat in the kitchen of the Royal Oak, leaning on the table and staring out of the small window into the night. For a while Agnes Hadlee sat with her, watching her, making occasional conversation. Soon it occurred to her that Karen was over the shock, and would now benefit from being left to her thoughts and her sorrows. The Quinns would keep their eye on her.

Mrs. Hadlee rose from the table, found her coat, said goodnight to everyone who remained in the lounge, and was then escorted to her car, parked nearby.

She checked the back seats and the boot but refused to be accompanied home. James was at the farm. She wouldn't have to walk more than twenty paces in the open. Besides, she was a match for any young man, axe or no axe.

Perhaps she had failed to grasp the full extent of the horror that was alone, and waiting, out beyond the lights of the town. Perhaps, not having seen Herbert's dissected body, she had failed to grasp the power of the beast that had once been Jack Seymour. Intellectually she could appreciate that a "maniac" was on the loose. Emotionally it had not fully registered.

She drove out of the town, her headlights on full beam. The road was clear, the trees seeming to lean eerily towards her as she approached. There were no lights on in the farm, but that certainly meant that James was in bed. She pulled off the road and onto the bumpy track that wound towards the farmhouse. She kept the lights on full, and nervously surveyed the surrounding darkness, but saw only the night-flying white forms of two gulls.

She pulled the car up abruptly.

Not gulls! Not flying! Shapes, figures, running across the lower field, holding hands, running towards the road!

She turned out the lights of the car, switched off the engine, and eased across into the passenger seat, peering hard through the window at the fleet-footed figures. Instantly she was sweating, her heart an annoyingly hard pressure in her chest.

It was a year since she had last seen them, but there was no mistaking the ghosts of that young, loving couple. The girl's dress flapped in a wind that was not in evidence, that evening in April; the boy's clothes were furs and leggings of a sort that had not been seen in this part of the world for centuries. A sword struck at his thigh, strapped to the wide belt at his waist. The girl's hair was long, plaited twice, and the braids flung about her shoulders as they sped across the field towards their rendezvous with some quiet place, away from the watchful eyes of their parents.

White as gulls, bodies not shimmering, but bright in the darkness.

The spectres of an ancient love, except that . . . something, some facet of the boy bothered Agnes Hadlee. She had seen the ghosts before, and others had seen them too. None had ever remarked upon the thing that she had noticed tonight for the first time.

It was not laughter, nor the anticipation of plump young love that twisted the boy's face as he ran. It was fear. The grimace of terror.

The couple were not running for their own ends. They were fleeing, fleeing for their lives!

Mrs. Hadlee shivered violently. The apparitions had vanished as swiftly as they had come, swallowed by time and night. She was suddenly very conscious of the blackness all around, and she noticed that the rear doors of her car were unlocked. Quickly she pressed down the catches.

Starting up the engine she drove the final hundred yards to the farmhouse, drew up close to the front door and let herself into her home. She turned on the hallway light and walked through into the kitchen. There was bread and cheese on the table, and she shook her head with annoyance. James *never* cleared away his supper things.

Taking off her coat, she turned and pushed the kitchen door closed so that she could hang the coat on the hook . . .

Her husband's blood-stained head stared blindly at her from the peg, and she uttered a scream that could have been heard for miles, backing away and into the table.

Slapping her hands to her mouth, she felt the blood drain from every part of her face and limbs. Clear-headed, terrified, shocked into a sudden silence, she stared at the grim trophy, watched the lower lip tremble as the door shut fully. The head fell from the hook and rolled a little way towards her.

She was half aware of the corpse, slumped in the corner of the kitchen, its chest opened, the rick dark organs spread across its belly. She knew that at any moment she would faint. The room had begun to swim. She wanted to shout her husband's name, to run to him; she wanted to cry, to die, to do anything to make herself wake up and see that this was just a terrible, terrifying dream.

But she was frozen to the spot, silent, rigid, eyes popping, watching as the kitchen door slowly opened, and the tall, broad shape of a man in grey entered towards her.

His hair hung lank and long, his beard was trimmed; his eyes were narrowed, fixing her with an hypnotic stare. He wore clothes like the ghost of the youth she had seen out on the fields, the same sort of sword hanging from his belt. His fur jacket was open to the waist and she could see scars on his deep chest; his arms rippled powerfully as he raised them towards her, and the bright-bladed axe glinted in the kitchen light.

It was a ghost, a ghost like the lovers in the field. It was insubstantial, unreal; it couldn't harm her.

It stank.

It made a sound as it stepped on the floor, and its breathing was laboured. The face regarded her with an evil leer touching its lips. A sound like a storm-wind blew from the throat and the face distorted, grew gaunt, became skull-like, the hair framing the bones like some hideous, decomposing corpse.

With the transformation of the face came the scream, and the figure took two rapid steps towards her.

Agnes Hadlee slung her middle-aged body to one side and the axe whistled down and split through the table. With a scream of panic the woman ran, to the kitchen door, to the hall, to the front door and out into the night. She ran until her lungs threatened to burst, out through the gate and across the fallow field; running, running . . .

The night air burned her chest with its frost. Her breath misted and steamed before her. Her voice was the whimper of one who is in an agony of despair. When at last her legs failed her, her body unwilling to move another inch, she collapsed to the ground and twisted round so that she could watch the slow, almost dream-like approach of the spectral figure.

— TWELVE

THE HUNT WOULD begin at dawn, but for Dan Brady there was much to be done in the hours leading up to the new day.

First, he erected simple, but hopefully effective, defences against psychic attack: he protected the lounge, the kitchen, and the large, main bedroom, where those who had stayed at the hotel would take it in turns to rest and sleep. Seb Quinn watched and sniffed suspiciously, dabbing his finger into the vinegar and salt mix that Brady used to protect against thought-attack, and recoiling alarmed from the heavy smoke from the herb braziers that Brady installed.

"You always carry this stuff with you?" Quinn asked, shaking his head.

"Always," said Brady. "I'm under attack constantly. I can defend myself against physical assault, but attack by the supernatural takes another sort of armour."

Quinn left Brady alone, saying only, "Well if it's the supernatural that threatens you, then in Wansham you'd do very well indeed to carry such things as those defences."

When Brady was reasonably satisfied that no simple, distant psychic attack could make itself effective within the confines of the hotel, he called Andrew Haddingham, rousing his friend from the beginnings of sleep.

"I need to use you, Andrew," he said softly, watching from behind that bar as Alan Keeton sat talking with Karen Seymour. Anita was trying to sleep upstairs, deeply depressed, still largely in a state of shock. Mrs. Keeton was up there too, still hoping that her husband, John would reappear at the door to the hotel.

"Use me?" Haddingham's voice was touched with the grogginess the man obviously felt. He cleared his throat and repeated, "How's that, Dan?"

"Go to my house. Brook's Corner—"

"Now?"

"Now! There's very little time. Ring up Angela Huxley first. Tell her that it really is a matter of life and death..."

"Yours?"

"Mine? No. But someone here, someone who might well hold one or two of the keys I need. And a woman's life too, I'm sure of it. There's a community in danger, and I need advice."

"From Angela?"

"From Ellen!" Brady felt almost impatient. "Ellen had researched things like controlling spirits, and defences against possession. I'm just a beginner, Andy. What I need to know from Ellen is how to *rid* a man's body of a possessing spirit, and *trap* that spirit. It's a destructive elemental, and very old. I have to get it out of one body and into something where it can't do any harm. Ellen *must* be able to help."

Haddingham paused before speaking, and Brady could imagine the sleepy cogs turning. "Ellen's ghost," came the voice. "I'll *have* to get the medium."

"That's your best bet. I noticed Ellen's shape reflected in mirrors, and the psychic writing approach might work. Get the question simple, keep repeating. There's a photograph of Ellen in the bureau. Look at it, try and remember her vividly. That much I know. *Get* her, Andrew. For God's sake, I really need some help here."

"Have you found them? Arachne? Anything at all?"

"Yes. They were here. Some of them may still be here."

"And your family?"

"I don't know. Marianna is useful to them, I've found that much out. But I don't know where they are. Not yet. Just do that for me, will you?"

"Sure, Dan. Give me your number. Then go through it all again."

A few minutes later Brady called Quinn over to him. "Get

your shotgun. We're going up to Kett's Farm." Quinn nodded and went to fetch the weapon. Brady walked over to Karen Seymour. "I'm going to fetch your car. Where are the keys?"

"In the room. At the farm. Probably in Jack's coat pocket. Do you want me to come with you?"

"No. Stay here."

When Quinn was ready, the two of them drove in Brady's car, out of the silent town, and to the farmhouse below Oldun Ridge. There were lights on, Brady noticed, and as he pulled up behind the Seymours' rented vehicle, Quinn said, "The front door's open. Look."

They sat quite still for a moment. Brady knew that something was wrong, every creeping inch of his flesh told him so. Together they got out of the car, and locked it. They walked to the Seymours' car and checked it. All the doors were locked.

Cautiously they crossed the yard, pushed the front door wider, and stepped into the hall. Brady gripped the army revolver tightly, glancing upstairs. Quinn held the shotgun in a ready-to-fire attitude, and nodded silently towards the kitchen.

Brady waited by the stairs as Quinn pushed open the kitchen door and stepped inside. A moment later there was a gasp of shock, and Brady knew that his worst fears were confirmed. When the landlord stepped back into the hall he was white, shaken and angry.

"Both of them?" asked Brady.

"Just Jim. Butchered, like the man at the church." Quinn came up to him. "He was a good man, was James Hadlee. That's a cruel death."

"No sign of his wife?"

"Her coat." Quinn looked back along the hall. "Her coat's on the table, and the table has been chopped right through. Looks to me like she made a run for it."

"Don't bet on it, Seb." Brady walked upstairs, pushing open the doors of each room in turn until he found the guest room. It was deserted, but he kept his back away from the door at all times. He found Karen Seymour's bag, and pushed her clothes and shoes into the small suitcase. If he had missed anything she would have to do without.

They turned the lights off in the house and closed the front door. Quinn pointed the gun towards the open fields. "She's out there. She must be. We ought to go and look for her."

"I know how you feel, but there's no point. If she *has* made a run for it, and got away, then I imagine she'll survive until dawn. If she's been unlucky . . ."

"Unlucky!" Quinn's anger surfaced suddenly, and he turned on Brady, his round face, normally so jovial, quite bitter now, his eyes narrowed with resentment. "He was one of us. James Hadlee. One of us, Mister Brady. The first, and by God, man, he's going to be the last if I have anything to do with it. The last to die like this! This little beauty will take a man's head off at fifty yards, and that'll stop this murderer taking another of us."

Brady could understand the passion, the fear, the irrational need for revenge. He said, "But it wouldn't, Mister Quinn. It's what I'm trying to get through to everyone." He spoke coldly, letting anger make itself transparent. "Blow him away and God knows what you release, and what happens to it. It might take you, or me. It might lie in the styke until some young couple walk past, and take them. You can't use twelve bore shot on a *ghost* . . ."

"He's no ghost. He's flesh and blood."

"And he's innocent. Jack Seymour is a victim. Believe me, Seb. You'll do more harm than good if you take lynch mob law into your hands."

Quinn calmed down slightly, glanced back at the house. "They were a good couple. People liked them."

"With God's grace, Agnes will still be alive. Come on, let's get back. You drive my car."

Back at the Royal Oak, Brady passed Karen's handbag to her, then gently tugged her to her feet. She looked haunted, quite despairing. Her dependency on Brady was growing, reinforced each time she heard him urge the local people to spare Seymour's life at any cost. She didn't like what Brady was insisting she do, now.

"Can you drive? Are you fit to drive?"

"Yes . . . why?"

"I've booked a room for you in a hotel, in Cromer. I want you to drive there now, and stay there until I send for you."

"Cromer! That's miles away."

"That's exactly right. Miles away from the thing that wants to kill you."

"Jack..."

"His passenger."

"I think you're wrong, Dan. Jack would resist any attempt to actually *kill* me."

She had convinced herself of the fact, ignoring his previous vicious assault on her. Brady shook his head. "I'm sorry, Karen, I can't take that chance. Think of your son. Think of your unborn child. Go to Cromer. You'll be safe there. Jack can't get that far, not for days. Please. Just do as I say."

She looked sorrowful, almost self-pitying. "You're going to kill him. You want me out of the way when you kill him." Sudden blazing anger. "I won't allow it. Jack's a good man, and a good father. You'll not kill him..."

Reaching for her raised hands, Brady squeezed her flesh until she winced. "I need him alive," he whispered. "I swear to you, Karen, I need Jack alive, and I'll do my utmost to make sure that no one here thinks otherwise. But we've got to find him, and soon. And you *are* in danger. Go to Cromer. When Jack is found, when we have him, I'll call you and you can come back. Not until."

And reluctantly, Karen Seymour allowed herself to be led outside to her car. "You even packed my things," she said, noticing the suitcase on the back seat.

"You sure you're okay to drive?"

"I'm tired. But I'm okay." A last glance at Brady, and she climbed into the car and drove off into the darkness.

A half an hour before dawn: men gathered in the hotel, then moved out through the town, towards the sea-bluff, the ridge, and the wide expanse of the styke.

The hunt for Jack Seymour had begun.

Seb Quinn took one party, of four men, out onto the fenland. Two others searched the gardens of the town itself, while the local butcher, a youthful, powerful man of twenty-eight, led a party along the shore. A retired army major named Fenwick stood guard by the tarpaulin-covered corpse of Doctor Herbert. It was his task to discourage any parties not in the know—the police especially—from discovering the body before Brady was ready for the full police alert that must inevitably occur before too long.

Alan Keeton had disappeared about an hour before daybreak, saying that he had "something to do" and would join Brady later.

Brady himself, armed with the revolver and well wrapped against the dawn chill, strode briskly along the road towards Kett's Farm, then along the field-edge and dirt track that led to the Roozie. He poked into each of the flapping tents, noticing that the contents of both had been thoroughly turned over, as if someone had been searching frantically for something.

Outside, he walked around the turf ridges that remained between the expanses of excavated ground, some of which had gone down to the post-hole pitted bedrock.

The last time he had been here, he was sure, there had not been any evidence of frantic, disorderly digging. Now in three places the ground had been gouged and torn up, the turf and earth-spoil scattered around the site, rather than being neatly stacked, ready for sifting. It was as if a dog had been scrabbling for a hidden bone . . .

Or a man digging for buried treasure . . . such as a talisman!

One thing that Brady noticed well enough: in the area where the damage had been inflicted, the turf had been split as if by a blade. It was a straighter cut than a shovel would have made. It was about the size of the viking axe that Jack Seymour was carrying.

Rising to his feet, Brady shivered in the crisp, dawn air.

You've had a good look for the talisman, but did you find it? Or had Holbrook found it first?

The distant styke was misty, although not densely so. He could see the figures of men, spreading out across the fields, searching the solitary stands of scattered trees, and the isolated barns and small farm buildings that were scattered almost randomly across the landscape.

It was as he looked towards the sea, and the grey distance, that he noticed Alan Keeton. The youth had seen Brady and was waving to him. He was near to the boggy pool where his father had almost certainly met his dismal end, and he was holding what looked like a long pole, with a hook on the end. Light glinted on the metal tip.

Brady waved back, wondering what the boy was up to, then realizing, almost in the same moment, that Alan was probably dredging the bog for his father's remains. The thought sent a shiver down Brady's spine, but he retraced his steps to the road, crossed the fence to the sea-bluff approach, and arrived among the trees, hearing the sound of splashing, and Keeton's grunts of effort.

Alan Keeton was breathless, sweating, and concentrating so hard as he swirled the boat pole through the thick mire that Brady thought he might be on the verge of bursting a blood vessel. "I've been at this for an hour," he said. "Thought I'd snagged him once, but it slipped." He stopped for a second, leaning on a tree and holding the pole firmly to stop it slipping from his grasp. He looked at Brady, "He's down there, I'm sure of it."

"Leave him, Alan. Just leave him. That pool's deeper than the pole."

"I know. But the body wouldn't have sunk all the way. Quinn told me that."

"Have you seen any sign of Seymour?"

Keeton swirled the pole and let the breath burst from his lungs as he tugged the hook against some deeper obstacle, but failed to move it. He relaxed again, and said, "Not a thing. I came here before first light, and all I could hear were gulls."

Distantly, someone shouted against the rising breeze. The voice carried to Brady, but he couldn't make out the words. Peering through the trees, towards the bluff, he could see a man waving, but the gesture was directed at an unseen member of the group which was scouring the sea's edge.

"Got something!"

Brady jerked his attention back to Alan Keeton, who was stepping back from the pool, dragging on the boat hook. His face was distorted with effort, drenched with sweat—and tears, Brady thought. It had come home to Alan, perhaps, that he was about to face the reality of his father's death, and the sorrow, and the awareness of the grief that would hit his mother, gave him redoubled strength.

Brady turned his attention to the rippling surface of the mud. The severed hand he had seen the day before was not in evidence, and he decided against mentioning it. As Keeton tugged, so the mud bubbled and heaved, the body rising towards the surface.

Brady frowned, peered closer at the pool. Why should mud bubble so? As if air were rising from the depths...

It happened so fast that Brady was left rigidly rooted to the spot, his clothes splattered with mud, his nostrils filled with the stench and pungency of decay. Cutting through the air came a shrill, unearthly screech. And rising through the slime, head bowed, arms moving slowly out from its sides, was the decaying corpse of a woman.

Keeton backed away, dropping the boat hook and falling to his knees, his face a rigid mask of terror, his eyes wide and popping. Brady raised his own hands before him, protectively, watching the hideous apparition almost in disbelief.

Mud and water dripped from the woman's lank hair, ran down the coloured dress, congealed on the jewellery that was slung around her neck. The head lifted, the mouth opening; squirming mud creatures fell from the parting lips, from the empty sockets of the eyes, and the shrill whine turned to a word; a drawn-out name, a haunting, eerie sound.

"Hollllll Brooooook! Hollll Brooooook!"

The words became shrill, the whine turning into a final, hideous shriek, the corpse's head bending backwards so that Brady could see the great gaping wound around the neck. A moment later there was silence and the corpse subsided back to the bog, turning slightly as it was sucked down. Keeton was rigid, shocked, staring at the pool; he was sweating profusely; only when Brady moved did he begin to respond, his whole body shuddering, a man mortally afraid.

Brady reached for the boat hook and snared the woman's body before it could vanish completely. He dragged it to the firmed land, and used the pole to turn it over onto its back. Almost apprehensively he crouched next to it, and reaching to wipe the mud from the decomposing face. He hoped that that last expenditure of energy was the final expression of the spirit. He didn't think he could cope with a further animation of the dead.

"What *caused* that?" Keeton stuttered, rising to his feet, wrapping his arms around his body and staring at the dead woman, not approaching.

"A last, agonized burst of life energy, trying to warn me, or tell who killed her. Holbrook . . ."

"The archaeologist? Herbert and Holbrook! What about the girl, Anita? And the other man?"

"I'm not sure about her. I don't think she's involved with what the other two were up to. But the younger man, Moss. Him, I think. Him I'm sure." Brady glanced towards the Roozie. Where the hell had they gone? Had they fled the area as soon as Herbert had been killed? Or had they left because of Brady getting too close?

Or had they found the "stone of power," and moved on to their next assignment?

He cleared the slime from the woman's chest, disliking the feel of her cracked breast bone, where the axe had struck her. She had not been subjected to the same disgusting ritual display as Herbert and the unfortunate James Hadlee. Across her breast were the necklets and amulets that had caught Seb Quinn's attention, when first she had visited Wansham.

And quickly, almost dispassionately, Brady pulled off the necklace that showed the severed, screaming head.

The mark of Arachne. She had been one of them, then, and her own kind had turned against her, when the ghost of Uffric had been raised and had run out of control.

Thirteen

THE NIGHT HAD been long and cold, and the cold had begun to etch his bones. But his spirits were high, a sense of exhilaration following his final, complete freedom, and the possession of this muscular, vigorous young body.

It wore clothes that were useless for the long vigil in the fens, and he had run for miles, keeping the blood pounding, the heat rising to the skin. It had felt good to wield the axe which he had induced the crippled man to fashion all those weeks ago. It had felt good to kill two of those who had betrayed him.

But it was Cedrica that he wanted, damn her black soul!

He had gone to the farmstead, where she had last been seen, and had killed the old man who hid there. But Cedrica had been nowhere in evidence. The old woman had run, given him a good chase.

But it was Cedrica he wanted, now. She had betrayed him. She had known all the time that she would hand him to his enemies, to die so horribly on the point of his own sword.

The woman had to die! He had waited in the void for so long, drifting in the nothingness, watching the passing of the years, waiting for the moment at which he might begin to resurrect from his deep earth grave.

It was a time, he could see, well beyond his own age, his own time. The homestead was gone, the land unfamiliar, bleak in a different way. There were strange structures in the distance, houses that looked more like the stone buildings of the Spanish than the wood halls of his own land.

It had been a long, cold night, crouched in the lee of a deserted building, battling, in his mind, with the confused images of the man whose body he owned now and which he would transform into a body more worthy of a chieftain.

Cedrica . . . where could she be?

There was a place . . . the vague memory of a building in the nearby township where people gathered to drink and to tell each other stories. The image was an image from *Seymour*, something he had seen, a place where he had gone. It was the sort of place that Cedrica might run to.

Cedrica . . . images of flaxen hair, plump young breasts, long, slender legs. Images of beauty, of fire, of passion . . . of betrayal!

And confused, then, with images of the woman he sought, of darker hair, and smaller stature, a woman with child, a terrified woman, who came from a land many leagues to the west. She bore the name *Karen*, but she was Cedrica, and he would find her now, and he would dispatch her as violently as her people had dispatched him.

She would be dead within the day.

He rose to his feet and peered through the dawn mists to where he could see men, spreading out across the marshes. They were hunting for him, he knew that well enough. But he was the greatest hunter of them all, and could adopt the attitude of prey as easily as he could be predator; he knew how to run, how to hide, how to breathe in moments of extreme danger. All of this skill he would gladly have brought to the girl Cedrica, and her family, Uffric and the others, along with the magic of the amulet, the talisman of power that he had inherited from his father, and his father before that.

The amulet!

He turned narrowed, tired eyes to the place on the ridge where the amulet was buried. He could *feel* its power; it lay somewhere below the surface, vibrating with energy, calling to him, but he could not find it. He had dug frantically all night, but he whom the amulet had destroyed had hidden the talisman well in the final, death-ridden days of the settlement.

He *had* to find it. He had to find it before others of this secret cult found it first. It belonged to *him*!

With the talisman he would become invulnerable in his quest for revenge. His time in the otherworld, linked to earth, yet growing in power, would make him unstoppable. The stone jewel, with its strange magic properties, the gift which he had brought for the father of Cedrica, would now be turned to his own use. The crippled man had dug well for him, had begun the excavation, but had not got near to the object.

But it was just a matter of time before he himself took back what was rightfully his.

The amulet; the girl. His gaze moved from the ridge to the town and his fist clenched angrily upon the cold, leather-bound haft of his axe.

Cedrica. *Karen*. A death to appease the bitterness in his soul, before he returned to the task of finding his property.

The body of Jack Seymour rose from its crouch, and moved lithely, swiftly through the trees, towards the boglands and dykes and the distant village.

Keeton was too tired, too shaken, to persist in the task of locating his father's body. He helped Brady drag the woman's corpse into deeper cover, then went back to the Royal Oak, to wash the mud from his hands, face and hair, and to make sure that his mother was all right.

He would join the search in a while, he promised, but Brady felt easier at the idea of the youth staying in the protected, locked hotel. He didn't know why; perhaps it was the thought that one death in a family was enough to cope with, perhaps because Alan Keeton seemed very vulnerable and might even be a hindrance to the others as they rooted out Jack Seymour.

Alone, Brady went back to Kett's Farm and thoroughly searched the buildings and out-sheds around, checking every animal pen and ditch before satisfying himself that only the remains of James Hadlee haunted the area. But Seymour had come here during the night, and there had had to be a reason for it. Not just that the farm was close at hand, Brady felt. He had come looking for Karen. He only had the legend to base his belief on, but he was sure that betrayal, and revenge, were the guiding emotions in the mixture of body and soul that was hiding out on the styke; a man, waiting for his opportunity to move, again, towards the person he had loved, and who had betrayed him, the memory of a woman, re-embodied in Karen Seymour.

He was glad, he was *very* glad, that she had taken him at his word, and gone to distant Cromer, to safety.

As he stood at the edge of the farm-yard, staring out across the fields, he heard the Hadlees' phone ringing, and walked back to the house, puzzled. When he picked up the receiver he found it was Tom Barlow, one of the group who had gone out across the styke. Ringing the farm on an off-chance, he was pleased to find Brady there.

There had been a finding, out on the styke, near to the grey beech. "Seb Quinn says you ought to go and look, seeing as you know most about this man Seymour."

"Where's the grey beech?"

It was about a mile from the excavation; he would have to follow round the ridge, cut across a cabbage field, across a brook, and look for a barn in the middle of the bogland.

Within half an hour Brady arrived at the tall, weather-damaged barn that stood alone by a single, lightning-struck beech, in the middle, it seemed, of nowhere. The styke here was a flat, scrubby expanse, soft underfoot, ridged and damp, and clearly carved into several levels where the rare deposits of peat—rare for this part of the world—had been taken up for drying. They had been stacked in the barn, brown clods of vegetable matter piled high against one of the walls.

Distantly, there was a bigger farm complex than Kett's. A minor road curved about the area, sheltered from sight by raised banks and a line of morose, wind-blistered oaks.

Seb Quinn was waiting for Brady, and there were two others with him, all carrying shotguns. Even as Brady arrived he could see that there had been recent digging into the peat for purposes other than gathering fuel blocks. The hole was twenty or so feet across, and had been dug down to a man's height, the turf stacked in the barn so that, from a distance at least, the digging could not be seen. The excavation was a hundred yards from the side of the barn and out of sight of the nearest farm.

"That's not recent digging," said Quinn, as he stood with Brady and peered into the pit; there was a shovel at the bottom, its blade rusting and dulled. "But within the month, I'd say. Now what the devil could they have been digging *for*?"

Brady said, "They? Who's they?"

"Why," said Quinn, as if it was too obvious for words, "the people that you're interested in. Them archaeologists, those two women . . ."

"Are you sure it was them? Couldn't the local farmer have been digging this to make a silo, something for the farm?"

Quinn shook his head and tugged at his broad moustache. "No, Mister Brady. He could not. Those doctors were seen out here on more than one occasion. The women were here too. In summer this is quite a popular walk across the styke. There's the path over there, leads up onto the ridge, through the woods. Quite popular. But come and look inside," he added. "*That'll* tell you who's been digging here."

The barn smelled of peat, and rotting wood. The floor was cracked concrete, years old and fast decaying.

Marked on it, in yellow wax, was a broad circle. Inside the circle was a cross, and in the four quadrants that were so formed words had once been chalked. Brady could hardly make the letters out, but he recognized them as what were called "runes," viking magic words to control the Gods and the forces of the realms of the Gods.

There were four part-burned black candles, and two bronze braziers, their contents a pungent smelling ash which was reminiscent of the ash left over from burning the protective herbs and woods that Brady used in his psychic defences.

He noticed, too, that the wall of the barn facing the pit had been deliberately sawn open, making a passageway just large enough for a man to crawl through. A line of the yellow, waxy substance had been drawn from the circle to where the peat began outside the foundations of the barn. Thereafter, the line continued as a cut in the peat, and when Brady reached a hand into the wound in the turf he discovered that the gash went deeper than his arm.

A connection between circle and pit.

Only one thought occurred to Brady: from the circle, men who were a part of Arachne had raised the ancient spirit of Uffric. The spirit was possessed of power, or knowledge, and Arachne planned to use that power in some way. During the first attempts at raising the spirit, innocent holidaymakers had been possessed; only later, a month or so ago, had the resurrection been fully achieved.

The reason for the pit seemed obvious. They had been digging for the body of Uffric himself, which must have lain deep in the peat, placed there by those who had betrayed him. Brady well knew that to possess the mortal remains would have given Arachne extra control over the Shade itself.

Perhaps the body had eluded them, and still lay deep; and now the ghost of Uffric had designs in the mortal world of its own.

As Brady peered through the gash in the wall of the barn, sighting back towards the ridge, he caught the flash of light on metal, up among the trees that were between him and the excavations of Uffricshame.

He narrowed his eyes, squinting through the morning light to try and discern more of that source of glinting brightness. But though it came once more, Brady failed to make out the figure that stood there.

And yet he knew, in his heart, that Jack Seymour was up there, watching the distant activity, waiting his chance, perhaps, to go seeking Karen.

Thank God the girl was safe.

She had driven to Cromer, not really thinking of what she was doing, or why, her mind a turmoil of concerns and confusion: for Jack, for herself, for their life in Canada, for what was happening to their family. The darkness enveloped her. The headlights cut a small, bright path for her as she drove along the winding roads, and she stared ahead, driving more by reflex than skill.

And in less than two hours she had pulled up before the hotel, with its bleak, sea view, and found the night-porter waiting for her, ready to carry her case to the room that Brady had booked for her.

She had sat in the small, stuffy room, listening to the silence, and the faint, mournful sound of the sea; even in the hotel she felt desolate, and her mood changed from confusion to disconsolate solitariness, and she cried.

Later, realizing that in Canada it was evening and that Chris would be home with her sister, she called across the Atlantic, and revelled in the sound of her son's voice.

They spoke for twenty minutes. Chris was missing her, and daddy, of course, and when were they coming back? Soon, she said. In a day or two they would both be home again, with a wonderful present for him.

Chris had been depressed, and not relating at all well to Karen's sister's children. He had been told off at school, which had upset him, and he was missing his own toys, and the company of the children who lived next door. *When* are you coming home?

Soon, darling. A day or two.

When she replaced the receiver in its cradle she just sat there and stared at it, her hand still resting on the warm, green plastic. The phone rang, startling her, and she snatched it up, hoping to hear Brady's voice. But it was the night porter ringing through the cost of her call.

Thank you.

What was happening in Wansham? What was Brady doing? Had it been a ploy to get her away from the area so that he and the villagers could hunt her husband down like an animal? She felt a knot of tension begin to grow in her stomach. *Images:*

Jack, his face distorted into a grimace of hate, running naked through the night, bleeding from her scratches, laughing, as if he had enjoyed the violating of her body. Jack, smartly dressed in suit and tie, arriving home from work, charged-up and excited. Jack, sweeping young Chris up into the air and running with him around the garden...

Dan Brady, so strong, such a strong-looking man, his pale eyes giving no access to the bitterness or love that might have resided deeper; a man with a mask, and the mask, she knew, covered an intense grief. But a strong man, a man she could depend on. He had said that no harm would come to Jack, and she believed him. But was he strong enough, was his willpower strong enough, to bend an entire village to his way of thinking?

Images: of fear on the faces of the people in the Royal Oak; the quiet determination of country folk that when things go wrong they will take the law into their own hands. She was an outsider, and so was Brady. A force of violence was loose in their village, and they associated it with outsiders, and maybe they'd turn against Brady as they would turn against her husband, Jack.

She paced the room, anxiously, frightened. If her body was tired, there was no way she could acknowledge the fact. Sleep was not possible for her. Her husband's life was at stake. Jack's life, her whole life, Christopher's life . . . everything was at stake. Everything depended on Dan Brady, and here she was, denying her own responsibilities, leaving her husband's life in the hands of a man she had met just hours before.

She was mad. She was madder than Jack himself. She had deserted him for the sake of her own safety at a time when perhaps he needed her more than ever. Yes: she could acknowledge that Jack Seymour was possessed, and would try and kill her, acting out some ancient grudge. But it was still *Jack*. Her husband was there, in the body, and he would exert control. How could she even *think* that the power of love and protection that was Jack Seymour would be totally swamped by the ancient spirit of a demon that had taken control of him?

If Jack was to be rescued, if he was to survive, it suddenly seemed to Karen that she *had* to be there, to face him, to talk to him, to remind the possessed man of what he had been.

And with Brady's help, the true life in the body of Jack Seymour would cast out the invading, violent elemental.

Without further thought she picked up her case and walked quietly down the stairs. She passed the porter's lodge unseen, stepped out into the cold night and made her way to her car.

It was well after dawn by the time she arrived back at the Royal Oak, and gained admission. The men had been gone for about an hour.

— FOURTEEN —

BY THE TIME Brady arrived close to where he had seen that telltale flash of light, there was no-one around. He had moved towards the bottom of the Oldun Ridge, with Sebastian Quinn approaching along the high path. Brady could see the portly shape of the hotelier, waving his shotgun in a way that meant: no-one up here.

Brady called to Quinn to come down to the fields. As he waited for the man's breathless arrival, he scanned the bleak landscape around, searching for even the slightest sign of surreptitious movement.

And it was as he stood there, staring distractedly towards the distant sea, that he saw the landrover belonging to the archaeological team. It was driving past Kett's Farm, towards the site that was the Roozie.

Holbrook!

With a shout at Quinn, who had stopped at the bottom of the slopes to get his breath, Brady began to trot in the direction of the farm. After a moment or two Quinn, holding the shotgun in his right hand, began to pound after the younger man.

"There's going to be one more death around here, Dan," he called. "And the supernatural'll have nothing to do with it."

Brady raised a finger to silence the panting man. They approached the wind-tugged tents. Brady reached for the shotgun and Quinn happily gave it to him. Distantly, carried by the wind, there came the sound of voices, subdued, intense.

Both men were there, and Brady caught sufficient of the conversation to realize they were talking about Herbert. They were puzzled as to why he had left the site unattended.

When Ewen Holbrook stepped out of the tent, clutching a large polythene bag in one hand and a clipboard in the other, he found himself staring down the double barrel of a twelve-bore shotgun.

"What the devil . . . ?"

"Move to one side." Brady waved the gun menacingly, and Holbrook obeyed, raising his arms slightly, his face creasing into bemusement. "There are no valuables here. I promise you . . ."

The puzzled features of Simon Moss appeared in the entrance to the tent and he, too, Brady called out into the open.

"What's the meaning of this?" Holbrook said irritably. "I dislike having a gun pointed at me. Where's Edward Herbert?"

"Dead," said Brady. "Your summoned spirit has turned against you."

Holbrook frowned. "My what?"

"Uffric. The ghost of the man who ruled here. You know full well what I mean. You raised his ghost, and the ghost didn't play your game."

Both men exchanged a glance. Moss's shirt was open at the neck and Brady could see that he wore a gold chain. He instructed Quinn to see what was on the end of the necklet, but there was just a small, gold cross. Quite clever, Brady thought. By looking closely he could see faint red marks on each side of the man's throat: marks consistent with an amulet having been ripped from him the night before.

"You were in my room," Brady said coldly. "You attacked me. You tried to kill me."

Moss shook his head slowly, meeting Brady's gaze evenly. "Nothing of the sort," he said. "I have no such violence in me. And why should I want to do such a thing? Besides, last night Ewen and I were in Cambridge."

Ignoring him, Brady used the shotgun to part the flaps of Holbrook's shirt. Like Herbert, he wore no talisman at his neck. Holbrook visibly stiffened, his face whitening, as the gun touched his flesh.

"What are you going to do? Are you mad? I'll have the police onto you for this."

"The police will come in good time. Don't worry about that." It was cold and exposed on the ridge. Brady said to Quinn, "Drive the landrover down to the farm. We'll meet you there. You two," he prodded them both. "March."

The three of them walked stiffly down the track to the farm buildings. Quinn let the vehicle idle along behind them, ready to give chase if either Holbrook or Moss should make a run for it.

As Simon Moss followed Holbrook through the front door of the farmhouse he slammed the door shut behind him, knocking the gun that Brady held. Brady heard the bolt slipped, and the sound of the two men running down the hall. Blind anger surfaced in him, anger for his family, for the dead man in the kitchen, furious rage that made him back away, raise the gun and discharge one barrel into the lock on the door. The door shattered inwards. Brady stepped across the wood rubble and walked swiftly to the kitchen, raised the gun at Holbrook, who stood against the sink, staring appalled at the remains of James Hadlee. Simon Moss stood by the back door, face frozen with horror and the expectation of death, as Brady pointed the shotgun at him.

"Come back here."

Moss obeyed.

"Who . . . what the devil . . . my God, who did this?" Holbrook stuttered his words, and Brady could see that the gory sight, and the sickening reek of blood and organs in the kitchen, was turning the older man's stomach.

"He did the same thing to Herbert," Brady said, and Holbrook's eyes widened with shock.

"Edward Herbert? Murdered? By who?"

"You've tampered with something a little out of your control," said Brady. "Sit down at the table."

"Get me out of here," said Holbrook, his face haggard, looking every year of his age. He ran a shaking hand through his white hair.

Brady repeated, angrily, "I said sit down! Hands on the table. Both of you. I don't have time to play games."

He walked round to stand behind the younger man, staring

across him at Holbrook. He quickly replaced the dead cartridge, snapped the shotgun shut again. Quinn remained by the entrance to the hall, watching Brady more than he watched the other two men. He held a handkerchief to his nose.

Brady raised the gun, rested it against the back of Moss's neck. The young man froze. Holbrook's eyes registered a satisfying degree of panic and fear.

"A night, four months ago. Before Christmas. You came to my house and you took my daughter, my son and my wife away. Remember it?" He pushed Moss with the gun and repeated savagely, "Remember it? You were there. You saw I was alive . . ."

"You're mad."

"I don't think so." Again he pushed the gun.

Moss said, "Before Christmas I was in Israel."

"I think not. You were working for Arachne. You helped kidnap my family, and left me for dead. But I didn't die. I'm on the trail of every one of you. I want to know where they've been taken. And if they're dead . . ."

Unthinkable. Unthinkable. They had to be alive still. The girl was useful to them, little Marianna. She had a special talent. She would survive for a while. Until the Roundelay.

"Who's Arachne?" stuttered Holbrook, eyes popping with apparent confusion and panic.

"Don't play games," said Brady quietly. "Where are my family? Were they here? In Wansham?"

"What can I say to you?" said Moss evenly. "I just don't know the answer to your question. I don't know who Arachne is. Uffric is a name I recognize, of course. Of course! But resurrecting ghosts is not quite my line. Whatever's going on around here, I really think you should understand that I'm not a part of it."

Brady felt frustration growing in him. The young man was too cool, the older man too practised in acting out the bemused innocent. He didn't care how much they denied, or played safe, *as long as they told him where his family had been taken!*

"I wanted to kill you. It was my intention to kill you. But I'll spare your lives for one simple piece of information: Alison Brady. Marianna Brady. Dominick Brady. A family that at least *you*," he pushed the gun barrel against Moss's head, "had a part in taking. Tell me where they are. That's all I want to know. *Tell* me."

"I wish that I could," said Moss. "I'm not going to lie to you, Mister . . . Brady, is it? I could make up a story. But I won't. I'm telling you. *I do not know where your family is. I had nothing to do with it.*"

"Nor did I," said Holbrook quickly, too quickly Brady thought.

"You're part of Arachne," he hissed. "This whole excavation is part of the Awakening, drawing on sources of more ancient power."

"The excavation?" Holbrook frowned, glanced at his colleague, then looking back at Brady. "We're excavating the site of Uffricshame. It's an Angle settlement, seventh to ninth century. It's quite above board, a genuine, sponsored dig. I told you this, before."

"Why were you digging near the grey beech? Near the barn?"

"The grey beech?" said Holbrook frowning; then he seemed to understand. "Oh, out on the styke, you mean. Well, yes, that's a bit odd, I grant you. One of Edward Herbert's hunches. We had two psychics visit us in the summer, then again about a month ago. We were trying to locate the sacrificial pool attached to Uffricshame. The styke, in the ninth century, was more marshy than now, and Uffric was one of the last semi-pagans, giving allegiance to both Gods, old and new. There's reference in a manuscript to 'God's Pool,' where his people sacrificed to the old Gods, or made talisman offerings. Herbert got the psychics in on a whim, really, to help try and locate it, and he dug a trial pit, but found nothing. I believe that's true . . ." He looked at Moss, who nodded slightly and said, "Yes. I helped with the dig, but it was a long shot. The psychics said they could 'feel' a presence below the peat. It didn't pay off."

Frustration surfaced in Brady, but he controlled it, feeling the blood pound in his temples. He wanted to kill, but he had to be sure that the men *were* part of the Sect that had caused him so much harm. It was not enough to hear it from the ghostly, haunted consciousness of one of Uffric's victims . . .

he had to hear it from the lips of the men themselves . . .

He said, "And I suppose a circle, with black candles and occult inscriptions is standard archaeological technique! Let me remind you of what you were *really* doing. You came here to raise the dead, to tap the power, or the occult knowledge, of a dead chieftain called Uffric. You partially raised the spectre last summer, and three people were part possessed, perhaps four. One of them was one of the psychics you called to help. One was an old man called Shackleford. One was a business man called Keeton. One was a Canadian called Seymour. When you finally raised the spirit of Uffric, it possessed Edward Herbert, and called the others back, to take back the remnants of its spiritual energy. Herbert killed them with an iron axe. He should have killed Seymour, but Uffric had decided to no longer play your game. Uffric wanted Seymour's younger, more energetic body, and he turned against Arachne. Uffric was once betrayed; revenge motivates him now, and you've lost control of him. He is using his power as much against you as anyone. You're not strong enough to compete with the old magic!"

Slowly, Simon Moss turned where he sat and stared up at Brady, through narrowed, almost arrogant eyes. "I've never heard so much nonsense in my life," he said. "I can assure you of one thing above all things, Mister Brady. No-one, least of all Doctor Holbrook, Doctor Herbert and myself, came here to raise the spirit of Uffric. You have misunderstood us totally, and you make me very angry."

Soon after, they found Agnes Hadlee.

She was crouched, frozen and terrified, behind a pile of empty sacks in a deserted barn. When the barn door was eased open, she stifled her scream and crawled deeper into the darkness, clutching her torn jumper about her shoulders, trying to lose herself among the piles of decomposing straw, and decaying wooden stalls. Huddled as far away from the door to the barn as she could go, she watched the tall, dark figure of a man enter and walk towards her.

He heard her pathetic whimper and came more quickly across to her. She screamed and tried to run to safety.

Strong hands caught her, eased her down. She scratched

and beat at the figure, only half aware that she recognized the voice that spoke to her so soothingly. "Take it easy, Agnes. Easy. It's Tom Barlow."

Tom Barlow.

Slowly she relaxed. Slowly she let the terror of the night drain away, and soon she was clutching at the man beside her, and weeping, crying out her husband's name, and letting all the fear transform itself to grief, relief, and tears.

She listened to the sound of voices, felt herself carried in strong arms. "Get on that damn CB. Get Mavis Quinn to come and pick us up. It's Agnes Hadlee. No, I don't know what's happened either. Just get that CB gadget to work, and get a car out here..."

"I don't like to leave you alone. Are you sure you'll be all right?" Mavis Quinn had hesitated at the front door of the hotel, looking at Karen Seymour, who stood behind the bar and smiled.

"I'll be fine. Really."

"Now don't you go opening this door to anyone, you hear? Only me and Seb have a key. Bolt the door, and don't unbolt it unless you can see one of us outside."

Karen Seymour nodded her head in tired affirmation. "I understand. Just don't worry. I came back so that I could be here when Jack is caught. I don't intend to go out looking for him."

Mavis Quinn hesitated for a second more; she was deeply uncomfortable at Karen's return, but also aware that a good friend of hers needed help, and fast. "I'll be no more than half an hour. Look out for me, now."

She slid back the bolts at top and bottom of the door, and stepped out into the street, to where her car was parked. Karen walked round the bar and pushed the bolts back into place. She glanced through the window to where Mavis Quinn was questioning silently, *everything locked?*

"Everything!" Karen called back. She couldn't help smiling. The woman vanished. Karen felt less like smiling than anything she could think of, but she felt secure and comforted by the attentions of the townsfolk, and of Brady in particular.

And she was back where she should be, ready to confront

Jack, to help him shake off the possessing demon.

She went up to the bathroom and changed her clothes, washing quickly and thoroughly, feeling instantly refreshed. From the upper windows she watched the sea-bluff and the distant styke, seeking for movement, hoping for a glimpse of Jack. She saw nothing.

Downstairs again, and she restlessly pottered about the lounge bar, cradling a weak gin and tonic, not really feeling in the mood to drink so early, but feeling in the need of some sort of stimulation.

And distantly, she heard someone call her name . . .

At first she thought it was Dan Brady, out on the street at the front of the hotel. But when she peered through the curtains, pressing her face against the cold glass of the window, she could see nothing but two older men, walking easily towards the church.

Again, though, came the sound of her name, called from such a distance that the voice was unreal; masculine, yet high pitched.

As she walked through the bar area and into the kitchens, the name came louder.

"Karen! For God's sake, help me . . ."

"Jack!" she cried, for instantly she had recognized the haunted tone of her husband's voice. She stood motionless in the middle of the kitchen, staring wide-eyed at the solidly built back door, and at the lead-bordered windows, with their view of the yard, and the back of a nearby house.

For a second there was silence. Cautiously she moved to the window and peered out. The yard was deserted, but the voice again, "Karen. I need help! It's Jack, I need help . . ."

"Where are you?" she shouted through the door, and from the corner of her eye she glimpsed a furtive, swift movement out in the yard. It made her heart race, a shock wave of fear and need passing through her body.

Jack crouched outside the window, then peered in at Karen, and she went to him, touched her hand against the glass, fighting back tears as she stared at his dishevelled features.

"Oh, Jack . . . what's happening to you?"

"I don't know, Kay. It's awful. I'm so afraid . . ."

His hair was filled with straw, and was wild, almost greased into a spikey, unkempt nest of tangles. His eyes were rimmed darkly, the skin of his face grimed and streaked with dirt. His finger nails were broken, and the palm he pressed against the outside of the glass, as if touching her through the window, was torn, ragged with cuts and grazes.

His shirt was torn badly. There were smears and spots of blood on his neck and chest.

"They're out looking for you, Jack. Lots of them. They promise they won't hurt you if you just give yourself up to them..."

"I've seen them out there, Kay," said Jack, his eyes wide with alarm, desperately communicating his confusion and panic to her. "Guns, pitchforks, iron bars. They don't *look* as if they intend to do me no harm. What do I do, Kay? What do I do? I need you!"

She felt the tears well up into her eyes, shook her head as she stared helplessly at his poor, ruined features. "I need you too, Jack. Chris needs you. But *all of us* need Dan Brady! Go to him, Jack..." even as she said it she realized that Jack didn't know Brady from Adam.

"Let me in first, Karen. I need to hold you. I'm so cold, so hungry. Let me in for a while..."

"I can't. I mustn't." She wanted to, God knew how much she wanted to! To hug him for a moment, to squeeze the strength back into his body, to feel his arms around her...

"Let me in," he pleaded, and she pressed her face against the cold glass window, letting her tears run freely down her cheeks as she watched his misery, his helplessness, the way he drew back a little, his head cocked to one side and—

Smashed through the window with an axe!

Karen screamed and flush herself backwards as glass showered her, stinging, cutting... the axe ate into the lead framing of the small pane, and Jack Seymour wrenched it out again, his face twisting into a demonic mask.

He vanished from sight. There was no sound. Karen cried, "Oh my God. Oh God..." and ran from the kitchen, dropping to a crouch behind the bar, peering over the counter, watching the front windows of the hotel for the fleeting shape of her husband.

Somewhere a door was struck, then struck again. The blood

drained from her face as she peered wide-eyed in the direction of the sound. Then, from the back door, came the sound of the handle being attacked and splintered, the door struck heavily, once, then twice, only the heavy metal bolts holding it in place.

Karen picked up the phone and began to frantically dial 999. She didn't know what else to do. Brady would be furious with her for involving the police, she knew. But she had to save her own life, *and* that of Jack . . .

The operator answered, clipped tones demanding which service was required.

"Police . . ." Karen stuttered, and then slammed the receiver down, her whole body shaking.

A window had smashed in one of the bedrooms.

Upstairs.

Someone came thundering down the stairs towards the door to the lounge. Karen screeched her fear, ran madly to the front door and began to rip back the bolts in a last, desperate attempt to escape.

The door to the bar was flung open, and the wild, hideous shape of her husband almost flew across the room at her, the axe thudding into the door beside her scrabbling fingers, only missing her because she swung round to strike at the hysterically shrieking figure.

Dead eyes blazed! The lips of the face parted wetly, the breath a stale affront to her nostrils.

She slipped to the ground, all strength gone, her legs like jelly.

Jack stood above her, legs straddling her body, and raised the axe to strike down and sever her head.

"Bitch!" he screamed. "Cedrica the Betrayer! Bitch! Whore! Your death at last!"

And he smashed down at her. She turned her head, eyes closed, unwilling to face him in these last moments of her life.

The axe hit the floor beside her. Opening her eyes she saw its bloody, iron blade, embedded deeply through the carpet. Jack was sprawled on the floor, on his back, his fingers clenched claw-like into the clothing and flesh of Dan Brady, who had his own hands firmly grasped around the struggling man's throat.

Through the open door of the hotel came Seb Quinn and several others.

Karen sat up, breathless, sobbing. "Do something!" she cried to Quinn, but Quinn shook his head.

"Brady knows best," he said, and Karen turned her gaze on the weird, frozen moment beside her, the silently struggling bodies of two men, almost completely stationary as some deeper battle occurred than could be witnessed . . .

Fifteen

THE LAST IMAGES that Brady carried with him into the struggle were of Karen Seymour's piercing scream of terror, the sound of bolts being drawn beyond the hotel door where he had been about to knock, and the sound of splintering wood as an axe thudded into that door on the other side. He barged through the door, hesitating only briefly as he registered the astonishing sight of Jack Seymour, axe raised, straddling his wife's sprawled body. Then he had charged into the possessed man, knocking him over, going down with him, struggling frantically as the spiritual presence in each man surfaced and entwined . . .

Brady felt his mind slip outwards, out of his body, then journey inwards, into the confusion that was Jack Seymour, into the darkness that was the possessing demon. Out of the one body, into the other, further and further, mind entangled with mind.

–This one is strong, stronger than the other. This one I want. Join with me, Brady. Join my mind.

–Not me. I've come to kill you, not to add to your strength.

–Join with me! I have waited so long for this sort of strength. You and I in one body, and with the talisman from the settlement . . . what power! What magic control over all who will come against us!

–I've come to rid this body of you. Too late. It's time to return to the mud of the fens. You're long out of time, Uffric. Your revenge is pointless now.

– Uffric! The fool calls me Uffric! He doesn't recognize me!

But Brady fought against the scornful, abusive laughter, reached deeper into the mind where the ancient ghost lurked, and slowly the darkness rolled back, and Brady saw the sea-bluff, and the wild marshes, and the prow of the long ship, beaching hard against the sand . . .

For an hour or more they had set-to a half mile off shore, swaying at the mercy of the low swell, observing the activity on the beach. Kraki was unhappy with the ploy, but Hakon Gudfrinarson silenced him. Kraki wished to be beaching the long ship, hard and fast against the land, then leaping into the cold Spring waters, sword drawn, chasing the ragged men of Uffricshame out across the marshes, before drawing a blade across their throats. Kraki was a War Monger, a farmer who spent more time thinking of conquest than of his own small homestead at the end of the deep chasm of Singasfjord.

"How can they respect men who sit motionless on the tides," he complained, "Like women nervously waiting for a lover? I say we assert authority now!"

His young eyes flashed, the thin blond beard upon his chin seeming to bristle with indignation.

Hakon listened to the murmur of confusion among the few men who had accompanied him upon this trip, then raised his voice, sensing the sea-swell of agreement for the violent Kraki.

"With this amulet," he raised the small curved head, fashioned out of skystone, and polished by the sorcerer Sigurd Odinseye; the face was calm, its eyes closed, a smile touching the strange lips. "With the power that resides in this piece of the stars, we can triumph by will alone. This is a mission of peace, of settlement, of mingling. Uffric's people have invited us to share their lands, and I for one know that the will of Odin is that we should avoid bloodshed. The amulet has told me that great prosperity awaits us all . . ."

"Whilst Cedrica awaits you. Aye, that's real prosperity." Kraki's tone was bitter. The girl was beautiful, and clearly it was Hakon, son of the Forkbeard, who would glean the greatest treasure from this peaceful conquest.

Hakon was young, but he was the son of a Chieftain; Cedrica was the daughter of a Warlord, the great Uffric Braetwaelda, son of a man of the same name, grandson of Uffric Raedwel, who had been the greatest of all the Anglian Chiefs. It would be a marriage between royal houses, a uniting of the blood-lines of enemies, and a peace would exist across the wide North Sea.

On the beach, Hakon could see the darting, waving shape of a golden-haired woman. He smiled, waved his broad-bladed axe so that it caught the dull afternoon sun. Light glinted on steel blades raised among Cedrica's kinfolk, the weapons of war used to greet in friendship.

Hakon felt love stir inside his heavy sea-clothes, the thick cotton of his trousers, the heavy, studded leather of his jerkin. The girl looked slim, beautiful; she awaited him eagerly.

"To the shore," he said, and the longship turned about, the land swinging across the dragon prow. Oars rose and fell, striking the gentle swell noisily, and the ship surged forward.

Within moments it had slid onto the sand flats, and the men of the north were leaping ashore, to embrace the folk of Uffricshame.

As evening fell the feasting tables were set up, and the men gathered to toast the success of the new friendship. The Gaulish wine was sour but on a stomach filled with fresh, fatty mutton, all drink tasted good. The great fire burned high in the middle of the hall, and cast shadows across the revellers, and across the pale faces of the women who watched. Hounds prowled about the dirt floor, snapping at the bone scraps that were flung from Uffric's table.

In the north of the land, the Norse raided, pillaged and suffered heavy losses themselves; the same in the south, a desperate struggle launched up the muddy channels of the rivers. Too much of the fair land was stained with blood; but not here, not on the marshes. Here a different conquest would occur, the welcoming of royal blood, and royal wealth from the northern kingdoms, to establish a new order, a people who would grow beneath the twin standards of the Norse and the Angle.

No blood, just the marriage bed, and the cry of blue-eyed, flaxen-haired children.

Throughout the feasting Hakon could scarcely take his eyes from Cedrica. She sat close to him, glancing sideways whenever she could. When she walked about the table to speak with Braetwel, her brother, Hakon watched the lithe way she moved, her supple limbs showing against the thin fabric of her gown. Her hair was fair, her eyes bright, her look at him one of hunger, of longing. When she spoke to him her breath was sweet, the firelight on her lips making their moistness gleam. She gently touched the amulet, with its smiling, enigmatic face, that hung around his neck. He longed to kiss her fiercely, while they writhed beneath the furs, interlocked in that most magic of unions.

Uffric nudged him hard in the ribs, winking. It was near to the midnight hour. "Has the wine softened your body?"

"Nothing could do that to me tonight," Hakon said with a grin.

"Then steal her away, Norseman. We do not stand on ceremony here. There's a stable set up for you behind the hall, new, sweet hay, and there are none who will disturb you tonight, since only I know of it."

Hakon rose from the table, swaying slightly as the strong wine took its effect on him. While the cheering and the laughing continued unabated, he moved round the hall. Kraki looked at him, angry, worried, his hard face still sharp with sobriety. He had not drunk the local brew, nor the Gaulish wine, and had kept one hand on his sword all evening.

Cedrica came to Hakon, and all thoughts of his irritable companion vanished. She seemed surprised at his boldness, but slipped away into the night with him, and hand in hand they stooped to enter the low barn.

The straw was warm and dry. They kissed lovingly and at length, and Hakon was almost tentative in his touch upon her thin body; thin in limb, yet full in bosom. When she tugged away her bodice he cupped the full flesh of her breasts, feeling the wide nipples stand erect and proud, indicating her deep desire for this man who would be her husband. She slipped down her skirts, then reached to tug at his heavy cloth breeches, deftly and nervously arousing him with firm strokes of her cool fingers. When he reached for her and pushed her down on her back she showed the first signs of fear, but spread her legs for him, and urged him to enter deeply within her virgin body.

Long after he had spent himself she kept her hands locked across his muscular back, pulling him rhythmically against her, experiencing the climax of love many times until at last he was proud again and his passion returned three-fold.

They were young and strong, and it was some hours before they were exhausted, and pulled straw to cover their cool, nude bodies. Hakon fell asleep against the girl's chest, and she stroked his sea-caked hair, and gently touched the swollen knots of muscle on his arms.

He awoke abruptly, in the dark of the morning, to the sound of a man's dying scream. His head ached, his body shook with fatigue, but he sat upright and shook the dizziness away.

The scream came again, a different man . . . Kraki! He could tell it was Kraki that was so agonized, and he swore loudly and reached for his sword. The girl, Cedrica, ran back into the low barn, breathless, terrified. Her eyes were wide and he could sense her panic, her shock, in the way she touched him, the way she breathed.

"We've been betrayed," he said, breathing the words, keeping his voice low. Shock coursed through his body. He touched the talisman on his chest.

"I've lost you . . ." she said weakly. "They'll kill us too . . . quickly, come quickly . . . there's only one hope!"

Hakon stood and pulled on his breeches and fur jacket. He picked up his sword and buckled it on. "I'll kill them first," he roared aloud, and made to run from the barn.

Cedrica grabbed at his arms, weeping as she implored him, "No! There are too many. They've opposed this union from the beginning. They've killed my father too . . ."

Uffric! Dead . . . the noble man, of noble blood, struck down by those who opposed his ways of peace.

"They're searching for us now," she said. "They'll kill us both. The marshes. Quick. Come with me. It's our only chance, Hakon . . . our *only* chance . . ."

So against his better judgement, Hakon followed the girl out through the compound, beyond the fires and the shifting shapes of the killers, and across the fens. They fled down the ridge, into the blackness, picking their way carefully along the firmer ground, darting behind trees and reedy growths, to give them protection from any who might have been following.

Kraki's death scream haunted Hakon as they ran. Kraki, who had known in his bones that betrayal was in the air. Poor Kraki . . . he should have listened to the man! Now he lay in the guest hall, head severed from body, breast bone split, Cedrica had said, in a cruel parody of the Blood Eagle, the ceremonial sacrifice to Odin . . .

"This way," she urged. "I know a place . . ."

He reached for her slim hand in the darkness, and ran with her. The night air was cold on his bare skin. His sword slapped hard against his thigh. She ran like a rabbit, fleet, darting, her skirts risen up around her thighs.

They came to the pool known as God's Pool; it was broad, gleaming in the starlight, lapping gently at the muddy shore.

Shivering, Hakon reached for Cedrica, and tugged her to him, hugging her. For a moment she melted against him, shaking with cold, with fear, he imagined. Then she pulled back.

"Where do we go?" he asked.

She reached to his belt. For a second he wondered what she was doing, then deftly, swiftly, she drew his sword from the scabbard.

"To hell is where you're going!" she said loudly, and Hakon gasped with shock.

In the darkness around them there was movement. A flint was struck and the dark head of a torch suddenly flared into life.

"No!" he cried, backing away from the five men he saw before him. Cold metal jabbed his back. He swung round. There were men behind him too, their spears held towards him, their faces smiling.

"Cedrica!" Hakon screamed, and her laughter mocked him from the shadows. She was standing close to her brother, snug in his grip, her head below his shoulder, her hand resting on his broad chest. She watched her lover, and she sneered at him.

Betrayed! Betrayed by the daughter of a noble man!

He took a quick step forward, intending to grapple with Braetwel, Uffric's treacherous son. But powerful hands gripped him, forced him to the ground. He screamed and struggled as the men closed round him. A hand jerked at his hair, forcing his head back. Rough fingers opened his jaws and he watched, yelling and fighting against his attackers as Braetwel lowered his breeches and urinated into his mouth. The hot liquid splashed and he gagged on the taste, but he could do nothing to fight the abuse.

Then Braetwel reached down and ripped the amulet from Hakon's neck, cradling the star-stone in his palm and grinning as he stared at it. "With this . . ." he began, then cried out in shock.

The star-stone talisman glowed dull red!

The calm face twisted, distorted, the eyes opening, the stone lips parting to give the appearance of a hideous, severed head. A deep groan emanated from the talisman, an eerie cry that rose in pitch until it was a shrill screech, that abuptly cut off. Braetwel dropped the amulet, clutching his singed hand to his chest.

Hakon laughed loudly. "You shall never use the talisman! It will bring destruction to you and your kin. For ever!"

"We'll see about that," said the man, and again he leered. "Turn him round."

Hakon was dragged around, his leather belt cut through and his cloth trousers and fur jacket torn from his body. Naked to the cold air, he screamed and writhed as he felt the cold point of his own sword pressed between his buttocks, then slowly, agonizingly pushed deeply into his body.

All his strength went. The steel burned like fire in his innards, the blood flowed hot and sticky down his legs. Cedrica laughed, reached out to touch his limp body, mocked him in the way she stroked his back and thighs, tentatively touching the embedded blade.

He was still conscious as he was carried to the pool and pushed below the surface. He had no strength left to hold his breath, and as the air bubbled from his lungs, towards the grinning face of the man who held him under the shallow pond, the last thing he saw from the corner of his eye was Cedrica and her brother, locked in a deep and loving kiss.

Sixteen

BETRAYED! ... BETRAYED! ...
Arachne has betrayed you! ... Arachne! ... Betrayed! ... Betrayed! ...

Dan Brady drew back from the grimacing features of Jack Seymour. Slowly the darkness shifted, his awareness returning to his body, vacating the violent and bitter scenario that filled Seymour/Hakon's mind.

Somewhere a phone was ringing. Brady could hear breathing, and the gentle murmur of voices. He became conscious of lying prone upon Seymour's body, his hands gripping the possessed man's hands, holding him down.

Seymour's eyes glittered with hatred, and yet the pallid lips moved: "You're strong, Brady. You're strong. Join to me. Come to me. Together ..."

Brady smiled weakly, shaking his head. "You're full of surprises. But no thanks." He looked round, realizing how strange it must have seemed, two men lying in such a close embrace. Seb Quinn stepped forward and took one of Seymour's hands, wrenching it down. Tom Barlow took the other arm and Brady stood up. He adjusted his shirt and ran a hand through his hair. Someone had answered the phone. Holbrook and Moss stood, morosely under the guard of another villager, who held a shotgun pointed squarely at them. The lounge seemed crowded with people.

Seymour began to struggle violently; but between them, Barlow and Quinn managed to yank the possessed man's hands behind his back, and apply two pairs of steel handcuffs. Quinn slipped a heavy iron bar between the Canadian's arms and back, and the man was effectively "defused."

Brady went behind the bar, took the phone from Mavis Quinn, and sat down. His mind was in a turmoil, confused by the way he had misunderstood the nature of the haunting...

A viking called Hakon Gudfrinarson all the time, not Uffric at all! The Stoneface in Anita Huxley's seance session had been the spirit of Uffric, a man betrayed by his people and by his own son and daughter. No wonder he was weeping. Brady had thought it had been Uffric that was the possessing spirit, but it was a viking Prince, who Arachne had raised, intending to use for their own ends. And Hakon had turned against them, turned against everyone, obsessed with his need for revenge upon the sweet young girl who had betrayed him...

Not a *father* revenging himself upon "the woman he loved," but a youth revenging himself upon that father's daughter.

The ghosts that had been seen fitted the pattern well... the young couple, running across the marshes, such a romantic ghostly pairing, and yet a reflected scene of awful treachery; and the Stoneface, Angela's weeping man, weeping for a people who had cast him out in such a brutal way, ending his dreams of peace between the people of East Anglia, and the Norse invaders.

Brady spoke into the phone, and was glad to hear Andrew Haddingham's tired voice. He had been up all night, with Angela Huxley, in the house at Brook's Corner, trying to summon the spirit of Ellen Bancroft.

They had succeeded. They had asked her advice.

Haddingham said, "All we could get was words, just four words: Blood. Iron. Death and Kiss. I think that ought to read "death kiss." Just that. Blood, Iron and Death Kiss."

Brady looked at the words as he scribbled them down, then shook his head. "Not much. Nothing else?"

Haddingham sounded weary and apologetic. "Tried all night, Dan. That's all that came through. Must mean something. There must be iron somewhere, that axe for example. But who gets the death kiss?"

"I don't know," said Brady, tiredly; but even as he spoke

an image came to his mind, and he smiled. "Yes I do!" he said. "Thanks, Andrew. See you very soon."

He hung up, walked elatedly back to the lounge. Karen Seymour stood there, arms folded across her chest as she sadly regarded the twisting, growling form of her husband. Brady put his arm around her and she moved closer to him. Seymour was like an animal. With his arms locked behind his back, he stood between the restraining grips of Tom Barlow and Seb Quinn, saliva dripping from his chin, his nostrils flaring, his eyes wide with madness.

Brady whispered to Karen, "In a few hours it'll all be over. I think I know how to get Jack back to the way he was."

Unexpectedly, abruptly, Karen turned to him and wept loudly against his chest, sobbing out her fears, her tensions. Brady let her weep everything out of her system, wrapping both his arms around her...

Then Seb Quinn raised an eyebrow: what happens now?

Brady said, "Get a team of men up to the Roozie. They'll see some untidy digging on the site and I want them to keep going down, but keep alert." He passed Tom Barlow the copy of Hakon Gudfrinarson's talisman. "You're looking for this. It'll be down there somewhere..." To Seb Quinn he said, "Get everyone else out to the barn on the styke. Where these two were excavating the peat." He nodded towards Holbrook and Moss. "Let's keep digging. There's a body down there that we need to resurrect."

"How do you know that?" asked Alan Keeton. And Brady just said, "That place was once called God's Pool. It was where Uffric's people made their night sacrifices out of the eye of the Church. The body that lies there is the body from which this possessing spirit came. There's a sword embedded in it. An iron sword." He peered hard at Seymour, who had calmed quite suddenly, and seemed to be watching him curiously. Brady smiled. "It's the way back to death for Hakon Gudfrinarson; the way back to life for Jack Seymour..."

It was late afternoon before a cry from the pit brought Brady out of the barn where he had been resting after an hour's digging in the peat. His shirt was saturated with the effort, his hands sore with blisters. He left Quinn guarding Holbrook,

Moss and the trussed, squirming, but tightly gagged form of Jack Seymour. Karen had refused to remain at the Royal Oak, and she sat with Alan Keeton, not talking, not crying, just very deeply in thought. Four men were in the eight-foot deep pit, now, standing back from their gruesome discovery.

Brady knelt by the edge and peered down at the grey limb that was protruding from the dark substrate. He felt a shiver of apprehension, a nasty judder of unease, as for the first time in a thousand years the body of Hakon Gudfrinarson came to light. "Clear the peat from it," he said, and after a moment's pause two of the men stepped forward with small trowels and began to expose the whole of the mummified cadaver.

Soon the whole body lay in view. The mouth of the viking was open, reflecting his last, desperate gasping for breath. The hands were twisted behind the back, and the black rope that had bound him could still be seen. His hair was beautifully preserved, flaxen locks that were matted around the screaming face. The eyes were half open. Except for the grey colouration, the man might have died a week before, rather than eleven hundred years.

Protruding from between the twisted, black legs was the rusting shape of a sword.

Seb Quinn was utterly astonished that anything so old could be so well preserved. "I've heard stories about things being dug up in the peat, intact and all, but I never thought to see the like of this. Quite amazing. You can see his scars, pimples. Good God, he could almost be asleep."

Using a piece of hardboard, the fragile corpse was moved from its thousand-year resting place and into the barn. Brady was amazed to find that the limbs were flexible, the skin very tough. They handled the body with care, but it was as if it had been buried just a few days before, the tissues hardly liquefied at all, except the one part of the face which had been downwards; around the left eye, down to the chin, the skull was exposed, in gruesome contrast to the glistening grey flesh of the right side of the head.

As the body was laid down before Seymour, so Seymour/Hakon began to agitate wildly, flexing against the cuffs that bound him, making loud, frightened noises through the gag.

Brady was unsure of how to proceed and he dropped to a crouch, running his fingers across the ice cold flesh of the mummy, touching and shifting the sword that was embedded between the shrunken buttocks. Each time he touched the sword the taping mouth of the body seemed to open slightly, as if a soundless scream were being emitted.

The others gathered round, Quinn keeping the two archaeologists under constant surveillance. Brady looked up at them. "When Hakon quits the body of Jack Seymour, he'll have enough memory left over to identify you for what you are. I've implanted the idea of Arachne betraying him in the mind. When Jack gets his release he may not have any memory at all of what's happened, but I'm counting on a spontaneous moment when he'll turn on the nearest member of the sect to hand." He paused, staring at Holbrook who looked wide-eyed and frightened.

"I had nothing to do with anything," he said. "You must believe me."

Moss looked frightened too. He kept glancing at the corpse as if anxiously awaiting the re-uniting of spirit and flesh.

"Bring Seymour," Brady said, and the struggling Canadian was dragged across and forced down beside the corpse. Brady drew out the steel blade he had obtained from the kitchens of the Royal Oak. Quinn loosed Seymour's hands; Brady grasped the right wrist and slashed deeply across the palm. Two men held Seymour still, watching the blood bubble and well up from the gash. Brady tugged at the iron sword, pulling the rusting blade partly out of the body. Holding Seymour's hand firmly he wrapped the man's fingers around the oxidized metal, then used his other hand, and all his strength, to bend Seymour's head close to the parted lips of the cadaver.

When the lips touched, so an eerie shriek escaped from one or other of the bodies. The sound filled the barn, echoed and drifted away across the peat landscape. A single, piercing cry of doom. Seymour threshed and struggled, fighting against Brady, but to no avail. The kiss of death, the breathing of life back into the mummy, continued . . . until suddenly Seymour was still.

Something that Ellen Bancroft had once said to him: it takes effort to draw the spirit from the body—there's a continual inclination to return, the link between body and spirit is very strong!

It had taken great effort to detach the spirit, trapped in the iron-impaled corpse of Hakon Gudfrinarson. Perhaps the iron itself had been the most potent trap of all, binding Hakon to the earth always. But the spirit had been sucked back with far greater ease than Herbert had raised it . . .

And suddenly the preserved corpse kicked, flexed its legs, then began to emit a low, gurgling sound which caused a greyish green slime to dribble from its mouth. Brady was horrified, dragging Jack Seymour back from the suddenly vibrant body. The greying mass of flesh flopped and twitched on the hard floor of the barn like a fish just flung from the water.

"My God," cried Quinn. "Shoot it now. The bloody thing's alive again."

Keeton had backed away in horror, his young eyes wide, his mouth gaping. Brady felt frozen, clutching the semi-conscious form of Seymour, watching as the millennial body rose uneasily, disgustingly to its feet. It stood six feet tall, the matted hair hanging lank about its shrivelled shoulders. The distorted grin widened; the dead eyes stared round the barn. The thin legs seemed almost incapable of bearing the weight of the corpse, especially with the sword dangling so obscenely from behind the loose genitals.

Hakon Gudfrinarson, surely powered by supernatural means, reached out a hand and staggered once, twice, towards the cowering man before it . . .

Touched the screaming man, reached to the neck, then flung itself into an obscene embrace, its flesh melting into the cold, pale, vibrant body of the man it regarded as having betrayed it.

Arachne. The youth. Alan Keeton.

"Get it off me," screamed Keeton, but the grey mass forced him to the ground, sprawled upon him, the embrace deepening, trying to block his mouth and nose, smothering him with its rotting flesh.

Keeton screeched appallingly. Brady let Seymour go and walked tentatively towards the struggling duo. He watched as the mummy's flesh seemed to deliquesce and flow, merging with Keeton, absorbing the youth, possessing him.

Keeton's look of helpless terror was deeply satisfying to Brady, who crouched by him and jerked his head round so that, for a few moments at least, the boy could speak.

"You then," Brady said. "You all the time."

"Get it off me! Help me, Brady, for God's sake!"

"You and who else? Tell me! Herbert? Yes, I know Herbert. Who else? Holbrook?"

"Not Holbrook," cried Alan Keeton. "I tried to trick you. I was told to trick you . . . *Get if off me!*"

What did he mean by that? *Trick!* Then Brady grasped it:

"The woman's body in the bog! *You* raised it. You made it say Holbrook's name. You misdirected me . . ."

"Yes! Yes!" screeched Keeton. "Do something!"

"How?" persisted Brady. "How did you do it? Are you developing mind-power slowly?" It would account for his exhaustion at the side of the bog.

"Being trained, developing . . . Brady!"

"It was you in my room last night. You were at my house. You were there that night, you were part of the group that took my children . . ."

"I was there!" yelled Keeton, and pain was beginning to be felt in every look, every twitch, every grasped word. The hideous face of the corpse was eating into his cheek, trying to absorb his face, trying to merge with the flesh so totally that Keeton would forever be bound to the thousand-year-old body of the murdered prince.

"Where have they been taken? Alison. Marianna. Dominick. Where are they?"

"I don't know. Oh God, it hurts. Help me, someone please help me . . . !"

"Where were they taken?"

"The girl . . ." shrieked Keeton. "The girl . . . Medfield . . ."

Brady was stunned. Campbell's house all the time!

"Melissa Campbell, then. She's one of them. Part of Arachne."

"Yes! Yes! She told me to make contact with you, find out what you knew . . ."

It made sense now. Melissa Campbell. She had almost certainly been one of the two women who had been around last month. And she had called Keeton soon after Brady had driven away from Medfield, telling him which way Brady was coming. Hitch a lift, find out what Brady knows, keep an eye on him. Finally: kill him if you can.

"What about Simon Moss? Is he part of it too?"

"I don't know, I don't know," wailed Keeton.

"Who else was with you that night? Who came to my house?"

"I don't know the names. The mammath. Just the mammath..."

"Who else? Who was the woman?"

"I don't know. I truly don't!"

"Where is Magondathog?"

"The north... in the north... I don't know..."

"What's 'roundelay?' What's the 'roundelay'?"

"Time of change. That's all I know. Time of change. Awakening... Oh God, get this thing off me! I'll tell you everything I know..."

"Get it off yourself," said Brady coldly. "Use your mind power..."

"I can't! I can't..."

"Where is Arachne now?"

"Everywhere!" screamed Keeton. "Everywhere!"

"Where is the mammath?"

"Gathering... oh Christ, it hurts! Kill me! Kill me, *please*!"

Brady straightened up and looked down at Keeton's agonized face. Once before, compassion had overwhelmed him and he had ended the last moments of agony of a man who had been present at the kidnapping of his family—but Campbell had been there by mind alone, a tool in the hands of Arachne.

Keeton had been there in person, one of the five.

Brady shook his head slowly. "Go to hell," he said, and watched as the corpse of Hakon Gudfrinarson smothered and finally drowned Alan Keeton in its liquefying flesh. The youth's hands ceased to clutch and scrabble at the body, his legs ceased to kick. Where the faces were joined the flesh seemed to burn and bubble, oozing slime. Locked in an eternal kiss, Hakon had taken his final revenge.

Karen and Jack Seymour were standing with their arms around each other, not kissing, not speaking, just standing with their eyes closed and the love and relief totally evident on their dishevelled features. Brady let them have their time together, then glanced at the lowering skies and sensed dusk approaching. He went across to them and at his approach, Jack Seymour opened his eyes, smiled, then shook Brady's hand.

"How do I thank you? It feels good. I can't tell you how good it feels..."

"I think I can imagine," said Brady. "It's not going to be easy... a lot of explaining..."

The Seymours exchanged a solemn, worried glance. "I know," said Jack. "I can still see myself killing them..." he shivered, then looked back at Brady. "What chance do I have?"

Brady couldn't really answer that question; except that there was a policeman, back in Buckinghamshire, who had been around Brady long enough to have had his scepticism worked out of him, a policeman who *knew* that around Brady, all hell literally could break loose. He would help. And the villagers, too, were not inclined to point fingers and accuse.

Brady went over to Holbrook and Moss. The young man eyed him coldly. Brady felt a distinct sense of unease about him; he was almost convinced that Moss was part of the cult. But he couldn't prove it.

Not yet.

He said to Holbrook, "I was wrong about you; I apologize. But I think you've seen enough to understand that your colleague, Edward Herbert, had been tampering with a lot more than simple archaeology."

"Yes," said Holbrook. "I think I can understand why you acted the way you acted."

"So I'll say goodbye to you, gentlemen." He looked at Moss, who smiled thinly, bowed his head slightly, and led the way to the landrover, parked nearby.

At eight o'clock that night, under floodlights, they found the sky stone, the dark, heavy stone that had been shaped into a face, then twisted, by supernatural means, into the screaming skull.

Brady held the hideous ornament and stared at it. It felt dull, lifeless. And yet it was a source of awesome power, a repository of magic that Arachne had hoped to unlock.

Now Brady had it. And he had no intention of letting it go.

"All that mess . . . just for this," said Seb Quinn, staring down at the talisman.

Brady just smiled. "Beyond understanding," he said, and added. "For the moment."

Epilogue

JUDITH CAMPBELL WAS surprised to see Brady. She opened the door just slightly, peering out for a moment and frowning before opening the door wide and saying, "It's very late, Mister Brady."

"I know. I'm sorry. I don't have much time..."

"You'd better come in."

He got straight down to business, wary to the point of jumpiness for any sudden move from the shadows. If Melissa knew that he was on to her she might be preparing to take defensive action.

"Where's your daughter?"

"Melissa? She's not here, I'm afraid. She left yesterday."

He had half expected that. *God, she had acted well. Brady had fallen for her bitter sorrow completely.*

"Did she go alone? Was there anyone with her?"

Judith Campbell looked puzzled, shaking her head slowly. "She was down here alone. What's this about, Mister Brady?"

"I need to talk to her urgently," said Brady. "Do you have her address? I'd appreciate it very much."

Mrs. Campbell went to her bag and drew out her small address book. "I'm sure she wouldn't mind me giving it to you," she said, as Brady wrote it down.

"Thank you."

He hesitated.

"Something else, Mister Brady?"

"Was there ever a little girl here? Did Melissa bring a child, eight years old or so?"

It was a desperate question, asked out of desperation. Mrs. Campbell had already been asked about the flow of visitors through her house and she had said, several times, that no children had been there in months.

Again she shook her head. "As I told the police, this house was our haven. We sometimes allowed small families to use the caravan, but not the house..."

Caravan? Brady hadn't known the Campbells owned a caravan. He had searched the house, and the sheds, walked the gardens from top to bottom. He had never seen a caravan!

"Where is it?" he hissed excitedly. "Where do you keep it? Not on the grounds..."

"Just outside," said Mrs. Campbell, startled by Brady's sudden intensity. "In a field, just beyond the lower gate."

"I *must* see it. Please. Where are the keys?"

Again, she dug into her bag. She passed the small yale key to Brady, who ran from the house, down the garden and through the gate. In the darkness the caravan was not at first obvious; tucked away below the trees, and being of a darker colour, it was almost lost in the shadows.

Brady approached it slowly, unlocked the door and, with his heart racing, stepped inside and switched on the light.

The place smelled musty... and slightly of cooking. It was deserted. The furniture was ramshackle and scratched, and in one room there was a pile of cardboard boxes and smelly mattresses. Brady walked from front to back, looked into the toilet, the tiny kitchen, opened every cupboard.

On his second search he found them, and he held them and wept bitterly, clutching the precious objects to his chest.

A broken pair of round-framed glasses. Granny glasses, Dominick had nicknamed them, and Marianna had been furious. But she had had to wear them whether she liked it or not, and Brady had adored her in them.

He held them up before him now, stared at the shattered lenses, the twisted frame. They had been stepped upon, or crushed, and the poor little girl was undergoing her ordeal in a universe of blurred colour and shape.

It made Brady very, very angry. Then it made him cry.

So close. So bloody close! And now she was gone again, twisted out of his reach just as his fingers had touched her.

He stepped out into the night. Standing below the stars, feeling chilled, yet burning with an inner resolve that made his whole body shake, he held the cold talisman and the glasses in his left hand and closed his fingers around them. Raising his fist to the sky he cried out loudly, and deliberately, "I *shall* find you! If it takes a hundred years, I swear to GOD that I will find you!"

TERRIFYING HORROR

The NIGHT HUNTER SERIES
by Robert Faulcon

Determined, remorseless, Dan Brady is the savage avenger of the demonic evil gripping his family. He is the Night Hunter. Pursued by the Stalker, tormented by a talisman, drawn by a demon-possessed Indian girl. One man against the monstrous legions of Hell itself!

_NIGHT HUNTER 0-441-57469-6/$2.95

_NIGHT HUNTER 0-441-57475-0/$2.95
2: THE TALISMAN

_NIGHT HUNTER 0-441-57478-5/$2.95
3: THE GHOST DANCE *On sale in November '87!*

Please send the titles I've checked above. Mail orders to:

BERKLEY PUBLISHING GROUP
390 Murray Hill Pkwy., Dept. B
East Rutherford, NJ 07073

NAME_____
ADDRESS_____
CITY_____
STATE_____ZIP_____

Please allow 6 weeks for delivery.
Prices are subject to change without notice.

POSTAGE & HANDLING:
$1.00 for one book, $.25 for each additional. Do not exceed $3.50.

BOOK TOTAL	$_____
SHIPPING & HANDLING	$_____
APPLICABLE SALES TAX (CA, NJ, NY, PA)	$_____
TOTAL AMOUNT DUE PAYABLE IN US FUNDS. (No cash orders accepted.)	$_____

Chilling New Tales by Modern Masters of Terror

NIGHT VISIONS

An innovative and exciting new showcase of terror—in which today's brightest talents present their darkest horrors. Each collection features three master craftsmen of startling originality and nightmarish insight.

__ 0-425-10182-7/$3.95 NIGHT VISIONS: DEAD IMAGE

Featuring spine-tingling tales by David Morrell, Joseph Payne Brennan and Karl Edward Wagner. Edited by Charles L. Grant.

Please send the titles I've checked above. Mail orders to:

BERKLEY PUBLISHING GROUP
390 Murray Hill Pkwy., Dept. B
East Rutherford, NJ 07073

NAME_____
ADDRESS_____
CITY_____
STATE_____ ZIP_____

Please allow 6 weeks for delivery.
Prices are subject to change without notice.

POSTAGE & HANDLING: $1.00 for one book, $.25 for each additional. Do not exceed $3.50.	
BOOK TOTAL	$_____
SHIPPING & HANDLING	$_____
APPLICABLE SALES TAX (CA, NJ, NY, PA)	$_____
TOTAL AMOUNT DUE PAYABLE IN US FUNDS. (No cash orders accepted.)	$_____